D1489804

Also by Ryan C. Thomas

The Summer I Died
Ratings Game
Monstrous (editor)
Enemy Unseen
With A Face of Golden Pleasure

THE UNDEAD WORLD OF OZ

L. FRANK BAUM
RYAN C. THOMAS

COSCOM ENTERTAINMENT
WINNIPEG

ISBN - 13 978-1-926712-17-8

PUBLISHED BY COSCOM ENTERTAINMENT
www.coscomentertainment.com
Text set in Garamond; Printed and bound in the USA
COVER ART BY SEAN SIMMANS

Second Printing

Library and Archives Canada Cataloguing in Publication

Baum, L. Frank (Lyman Frank), 1856-1919
    The undead world of Oz : L. Frank Baum's beloved tale complete with
zombies and monsters / L. Frank Baum, Ryan C. Thomas.

ISBN 978-1-926712-17-8

    I. Thomas, Ryan C., 1975- II. Title.

PZ7.B327Wi 2009   813'.4   C2009-905600-3

For Jack and Lily, who will always
have five hundred hearts in my book.

Contents

1. The Cyclone 1
2. The Council with the Munchkins 5
3. How Dorothy Saved the Scarecrow 13
4. The Road Through the Undead Forest 20
5. The Rescue of the Tin Woodman 25
6. The Cowardly Lion 31
7. The Journey to the Great Oz 37
8. The Deadly Poppy Field 45
9. The Queen of the Field Mice 50
10. The Guardian of the Gates 55
11. The Emerald City of Oz 62
12. The Search for the Wicked Witch 71
13. The Rendezvous 83
14. The Battle of the Winged Monkeys 86
15. The Discovery of Oz, the Terrible 93
16. The Magic Art of the Great Humbug 101
17. How the Balloon Was Launched 104
18. Away to the South 109
19. Attacked by the Fighting Trees 113
20. The Dainty China Country 117
21. The Lion Becomes the King of Beasts 122
22. The Country of the Quadlings 126
23. Glinda the Good Witch Grants Dorothy's Wish 129
24. The Battle for Oz 132
25. Home Again 139

THE UNDEAD WORLD OF OZ

1

The Cyclone

DOROTHY LIVED IN the midst of the great Kansas prairies, with Uncle Henry, who was a farmer, and Aunt Em, who was the farmer's wife. Their house was small, for the lumber to build it had to be carried by wagon many miles. There were four walls, a floor and a roof, which made one room; and this room contained a rusty looking cookstove, a cupboard for the dishes, a table, three or four chairs, and the beds. Uncle Henry and Aunt Em had a big bed in one corner, and Dorothy a little bed in another corner. There was no garret at all, and no cellar—except a small hole dug in the ground, called a cyclone cellar, where the family could go in case one of those great whirlwinds arose, mighty enough to crush any building in its path. It was reached by a trap door in the middle of the floor, from which a ladder led down into the small, dark hole.

When Dorothy stood in the doorway and looked around, she could see nothing but the great gray prairie on every side. Not a tree nor a house broke the broad sweep of flat country that reached to the edge of the sky in all directions. The sun had baked the plowed land into a gray mass, with little cracks running through it. Even the grass was not green, for the sun had burned the tops of the long blades until they were the same gray color to be seen everywhere. Once the house had been painted, but the sun blistered the paint and the rains washed it away, and now the house was as dull and gray as everything else.

On some days Dorothy felt she was living in a graveyard rather than a farm. Where the charred land no longer grew, patches of deep gray dirt stretched to the horizon like a slab of cement. What could grow on such land, she wondered. There were no living roots under the soil, just worms and other insects looking for their own food.

When Aunt Em came there to live she was a young, pretty wife. The sun and wind had changed her, too. They had taken the sparkle from her eyes and left them a sober gray; they had taken the red from her cheeks and lips, and they were gray also. She was thin and gaunt, and never smiled now, and her eyes had gone as sallow as the setting sun. Every morning, after fixing a meager breakfast, she would shuffle about the house, moaning, hoping the land would become fallow once more. Dorothy avoided her on these days, for her aunt looked like something near death, and the sound of her hungry, smacking lips, desperate for food, made Dorothy's spine tingle.

When Dorothy, who was an orphan, first came to her, Aunt Em had been so startled by the child's laughter that she would scream and press her hand upon her heart whenever Dorothy's merry voice reached her ears; and she still looked at the little girl with wonder that she could find anything to laugh at.

Uncle Henry never laughed. He worked hard from morning till night and did not know what joy was. He was gray also, from his long beard to his rough boots, and he looked stern and solemn, and rarely spoke. Deep blue veins cut across his forehead like tiny rivers; tiny rivers that Dorothy wished would cut through the gray land around her home. Maybe then there would be crops. Maybe then she wouldn't have to stare at her aunt and uncle's thin frames and hungry bellies.

It was Toto that made Dorothy laugh, and saved her from growing as gray and depressing as her other surroundings. Toto was not gray; he was a little black dog, with long silky hair and small black eyes that twinkled merrily on either side of his funny, wee nose. Toto played all day long, and Dorothy played with him, and loved him dearly.

Today, however, they were not playing. Uncle Henry sat upon the doorstep and looked anxiously at the sky, which was even grayer than usual. Dorothy stood in the door with Toto in her arms, and looked at the sky too. Aunt Em was washing the dishes.

From the far north they heard a low wail of the wind, and Uncle Henry and Dorothy could see where the long grass bowed in waves before the coming storm. There now came a sharp whistling in the air from the south, and as they turned their eyes that way they saw ripples in the grass coming from that direction also.

Suddenly Uncle Henry stood up.

"There's a cyclone coming, Em," he called to his wife. "I'll go look after the stock." Then he ran toward the sheds where the cows and horses were kept, all of them as thin and gray as the land they grazed off of.

Aunt Em dropped her work and came to the door. One glance told her of the danger close at hand.

"Quick, Dorothy!" she screamed. "Run for the cellar!"

Toto jumped out of Dorothy's arms and hid under the bed, and the girl started to get him. Aunt Em, badly frightened, threw open the trap door in the floor and climbed down the ladder into the small, dark hole. It was down there that Aunt Em slaughtered the pigs, when they were big enough to eat. Even now Dorothy saw the blood stains on the walls in that basement, and dreaded entering it. She saw a cleaver hanging near the trap door and wondered what would happen if it flew off its hook and caught her in the throat.

"Dorothy, hurry!" Aunt Em shouted.

Dorothy caught Toto at last and started to follow her aunt. When she was halfway across the room there came a great shriek from the wind, and the house shook so hard that she lost her footing and sat down suddenly upon the floor.

Then a strange thing happened.

The house whirled around two or three times and rose slowly through the air. Dorothy felt as if she were going up in a balloon.

The north and south winds met where the house stood, and made it the exact center of the cyclone. In the middle of a cyclone the air is generally still, but the great pressure of the wind on every side of the house raised it up higher and higher, until it was at the very top of the cyclone; and there it remained and was carried miles and miles away as easily as you could carry a feather.

It was very dark, and the wind howled horribly around her, but Dorothy found she was riding quite easily. After the first few whirls around, and one other time when the house tipped badly, she felt as if she were being rocked gently, like a baby in a cradle.

Toto did not like it. He ran about the room, now here, now there, barking loudly; but Dorothy sat quite still on the floor and waited to see what would happen.

Through the trap door she could see things spinning in the cyclone beneath her. A bicycle, a small cow, a wheelbarrow and even a person. The person was nothing but a skeleton now, wrapped in torn clothing, long since dead. Dorothy knew that early settlers buried their loved ones in the ground all around Kansas. Uncle Henry had told her this. The cyclone must have wrenched this one from a low grave.

The body flew closer to the trap door, the arms waving as if alive. Its teeth clicked together as the wind gusted through its jaws. Its gray skull smacked the underside of the house and then was gone.

"How terrifying," Dorothy said, and hugged Toto for safety.

The house continued to twirl and the wind continued to howl.

Eventually Dorothy set Toto down and lay on her belly, watching the storm through the trap door.

Once Toto got too near the open trap door, and fell in; and at first the little girl thought she had lost him. But soon she saw one of his ears sticking up through the hole, for the strong pressure of the air was keeping him up so that he could not fall. She crept to the hole, caught Toto by the ear, and dragged him into the room again, afterward closing the trap door so that no more accidents could happen. Hour after hour passed away, and slowly Dorothy got over her fright; but she felt quite lonely, and the wind shrieked so loudly all about her that she nearly became deaf. At first she had wondered if she would be dashed to pieces when the house fell again; but as the hours passed and nothing terrible happened, she stopped worrying and resolved to wait calmly and see what the future would bring. At last she crawled over the swaying floor to her bed, and lay down upon it; and Toto followed and lay down beside her.

In spite of the swaying of the house and the wailing of the wind, Dorothy soon closed her eyes and fell fast asleep.

2
The Council with the Munchkins

SHE WAS AWAKENED by a shock, so sudden and severe that if Dorothy had not been lying on the soft bed she might have been hurt. As it was, the jar made her catch her breath and wonder what had happened; and Toto put his cold little nose into her face and whined dismally. Dorothy sat up and noticed that the house was not moving; nor was it dark, for the bright sunshine came in at the window, flooding the little room. She sprang from her bed and with Toto at her heels ran and opened the door.

The little girl gave a cry of amazement and looked about her, her eyes growing bigger and bigger at the wonderful sights she saw.

The cyclone had set the house down very gently—for a cyclone—in the midst of a country of marvelous beauty. There were lovely patches of greensward all about, with stately trees bearing rich and luscious fruits. Banks of gorgeous flowers were on every hand, and birds with rare and brilliant plumage sang and fluttered in the trees and bushes. A little way off was a small brook, rushing and sparkling along between green banks, and murmuring in a voice very grateful to a little girl who had lived so long on the dry, gray prairies.

While she stood looking eagerly at the strange and beautiful sights, she noticed coming toward her a group of the queerest people she had ever seen. They were not as big as the grown folk she had always been used to; but neither were they very small. In fact, they seemed about as tall as Dorothy, who was a well-grown child for her age, although they were, so far as looks go, many years older.

Three were men and one a woman, and all were oddly dressed. They wore round hats that rose to a small point a foot above their heads, with little bells around the brims that tinkled sweetly as they moved. The hats of the men were blue; the little woman's hat was white, and she wore a white gown that hung in pleats from her shoulders. Over it were sprinkled little stars that glistened in the sun like diamonds. The men were dressed in blue, of the same shade as their hats, and wore well-polished boots with a deep roll of blue at the tops. The men, Dorothy thought, were about as old as Uncle Henry, for two of them had beards. But the little woman was doubtless much older. Her face was covered with wrinkles, her hair was nearly white, and she walked rather stiffly.

When these people drew near the house where Dorothy was standing in the doorway, they paused and whispered among themselves, as if afraid to come farther. But the little old woman walked up to Dorothy, made a low bow and said, in a sweet voice:

"You are welcome, most noble Sorceress, to the land of the Munchkins. We are so grateful to you for having killed the Wicked Witch of the East, and for setting our people free from the horrible plague she has beset upon us."

Dorothy listened to this speech with wonder. What could the little woman possibly mean by calling her a sorceress, and saying she had killed the Wicked Witch of the East? Dorothy was an innocent, harmless little girl, who had been carried by a cyclone many miles from home; and she had never killed anything in all her life.

But the little woman evidently expected her to answer; so Dorothy said, with hesitation, "You are very kind, but there must be some mistake. I have not killed anything."

"Your house did, anyway," replied the little old woman with a laugh, "and that is the same thing. See!" she continued, pointing to the corner of the house. "There are her two feet, still sticking out from under a block of wood."

Dorothy looked, and gave a little cry of fright. There, indeed, just under the corner of the great beam the house rested on, two feet were sticking out, shod in silver shoes with pointed toes.

"Oh, dear! Oh, dear!" cried Dorothy, clasping her hands together in dismay. "The house must have fallen on her. Whatever shall we do?"

"There is nothing to be done," said the little woman calmly.

"But who was she?" asked Dorothy.

"She was the Wicked Witch of the East, as I said," answered the little woman. "She has held all the Munchkins in bondage for many years, making them slave for her night and day. And just the other day, to show that no Munchkin could ever escape her even in death, she set a plague upon us."

"What sort of plague," Dorothy asked.

"The Wicked Witch of the East has raised all of the dead Munchkins from the land. Now they attack their former friends and families. It is most horrible!"

"From the dead? But why do they attack?"

"For our brains," said one of the little men in blue. "They want to eat our brains."

"The Wicked Witch has given them an insatiable hunger," confirmed the next little blue man.

"How gross," Dorothy replied. "But then, I'm not sure who you mean by Munchkins."

"They are the people who live in this land of the East where the Wicked Witch ruled."

"Are you a Munchkin?" asked Dorothy.

"No, but I am their friend, although I live in the land of the North. When they saw the Witch of the East was dead the Munchkins sent a swift messenger to me, and I came at once. I am the Witch of the North."

"Oh, gracious!" cried Dorothy. "Are you a real witch?"

"Yes, indeed," answered the little woman. "But I am a good witch, and the people love me. I am not as powerful as the Wicked Witch was who ruled here, or I should have set the people free myself."

"But I thought all witches were wicked," said the girl, who was half frightened at facing a real witch.

"Oh, no, that is a great mistake. There were only four witches in all the Land of Oz, and two of them, those who live in the North and the South, are good witches. I know this is true, for I am one of them myself, and cannot be mistaken. Those who dwelt in the East and the West were, indeed, wicked witches; but now that you have killed one of them, there is but one Wicked Witch in all the Land of Oz—the one who lives in the West."

"We should not stay outside long," said one of the other small men. "The undead are close by. They will eat our brains if they see us."

"Too late," said his fellow wee man in blue. "Here they come!"

Dorothy watched as several Munchkins, each as gray as her aunt and uncle, shambled forward from the river bank. They held their arms out as they moved and whined with high-pitched voices that made her think of the way Toto whined when he was hungry.

"Braaiins," they moaned. "Small braaaiiins."

"Let me handle this," said the Good Witch. She raised her wand and let a bolt of light shoot forth from the tip. The light hit the shambling dead Munchkins and blew their heads clean off. Dorothy stifled a squeak as brains and gristle streamed through the air like birthday party favors.

"But there are more," cried the Munchkins next to Dorothy.

And they were right. When Dorothy turned to look behind her, a collection of shuffling gray Munchkins crested the tiny hill between the small homes, trampling the beautiful flowers as they came. From their tiny Munchkin mouths dripped ribbons of red. Toto barked and started to run toward them, but Dorothy grabbed him. "No, Toto, you stay with me," she said. "He's always trying to protect me."

"This way, my dear," the Witch said, offering her hand. Dorothy grabbed it and together they floated on a cushion of air to one of the tiny dome-shaped houses that lined the narrow streets. They entered and Dorothy noticed how tiny all the furniture was. It was almost like a big doll house. The Witch of the North raised her wand and created an invisible shield around the house. Only when Dorothy touched it could she a tiny sparkling that told her where it was. The Witch touched it as well, as if admiring her own handiwork, and then she leaned against it, looking a bit tired. "This shield is powerful, but it drains me for some time. Alas, we will be safe here for now."

From inside the house, Dorothy watched as many more Munchkin men appeared from the surrounding homes, each holding a small rifle.

Tiny as the guns were, the blue Munchkins managed to hold off the advancing wave of gray, rotted Munchkin corpses. Many bullets hit home in the delicate skulls of the miniature undead, and there was much blood on the ground now. Dorothy was sad when she saw one of the Munchkins who had greeted her get taken by surprise from behind by a rather fat undead Munchkin. The beefy walking corpse sank its rotted yellow teeth into the nice man's neck and tore loose a cut of meat that would make Aunt Em salivate.

"Do not let me turn into—" the little man shouted, but his voice was cut off as one of his friends shot him in the head. *Everything about them is so small*, Dorothy thought. Their guns, their hands, even their body parts, which were strewn about the sidewalks in little puddles of Munchkin stew.

The battle was over very quickly, as tiny Munchkin bullets tore the tiny heads off of the undead. When it was over, the blue Munchkins were very sad, and dragged the dead bodies of their friends down to the river and began to bury them.

"There will be another wave later," the Good Witch explained. "The Munchkins have lived here for many centuries, and the dead are abundant. We have not been able to stop this blight."

"Surely you can just shoot them all, like I just saw," Dorothy said.

Alas, the Witch shook her head. "No, their numbers are too many, and when they come, they come as a swarm and we must keep moving to new Munchkin towns. At least now, thanks to you, the Wicked Witch of the East can no longer make new plagues."

"But you are a witch, too. Can't you use magic?" Toto barked to show he was thinking the same thing, for Toto was a smart dog and this witch was not making sense.

"Of course, little sorceress, but I cannot fight another witch's curse."

"That seems awfully inconvenient," Dorothy said.

"It comes with the territory, my girl."

"But," said Dorothy, after a moment's thought, "I'm still confused. Aunt Em has told me that the witches were all dead—years and years ago."

"Who is Aunt Em?" inquired the little old woman.

"She is my aunt who lives in Kansas, where I came from."

The Witch of the North seemed to think for a time, with her head bowed and her eyes upon the ground. Then she looked up and said, "I do not know where Kansas is, for I have never heard that country mentioned before. But tell me, is it a civilized country, do the dead walk the streets?"

"Oh, yes," replied Dorothy, "it is civilized. We have no walking dead." Just then Dorothy thought of the corpse she'd seen below the house as it flew in the cyclone. "At least not that are truly living again," she added.

"Then that accounts for it. In the civilized countries I believe there are no witches left, nor wizards, nor sorceresses, nor magicians. Therefore, no undead plagues. But, you see, the Land of Oz has never been civilized, for we are cut off from all the rest of the world. Therefore we still have witches and wizards and now this horrible curse amongst us."

"Who are the wizards?" asked Dorothy.

"Oz himself is the Great Wizard," answered the Witch, sinking her voice to a whisper. "He is more powerful than all the rest of us together. He lives in the City of Emeralds."

Dorothy was going to ask another question, but just then the Munchkins, who had been standing outside, gave a loud shout and urged Dorothy and the Witch to join them. When Dorothy and the Witch were outside, the munchkins pointed to the corner of Dorothy's house where the Wicked Witch had been lying.

"What is it?" asked the little old woman, and looked, and began to laugh. The feet of the dead Witch had disappeared entirely, and nothing was left but the silver shoes.

"She was so old," explained the Witch of the North, "that she dried up quickly in the sun. That is the end of her. But the silver shoes are yours, and you shall have them to wear." She reached down and picked up the shoes, and after shaking the blood and bits of flesh off of them handed them to Dorothy.

"The Witch of the East was proud of those silver shoes," said one of the Munchkins, his face coated in a collection of meaty gore that belonged in one of Aunt Em's seasonal pies, "and there is some charm connected with them; but what it is we never knew."

Dorothy carried the shoes into the house and placed them on the table. Then she came out again to the Munchkins and said:

"I am anxious to get back to my aunt and uncle, for I am sure they will worry about me. Can you help me find my way?"

The Munchkins and the Witch first looked at one another, and then at Dorothy, and then shook their heads.

"At the East, not far from here," said one, "there is a great desert, and none could live to cross it."

"It is the same at the South," said another, "for I have been there and seen it. The South is the country of the Quadlings."

"I am told," said the third man, "that it is the same at the West. And that country, where the Winkies live, is ruled by the Wicked Witch of the West, who would make you her slave if you passed her way."

"The North is my home," said the old lady, "and at its edge is the same great desert that surrounds this Land of Oz. I'm afraid, my dear, you will have to live with us."

Dorothy began to sob at this, for she felt lonely among all these strange people and was not fond of the dead Munchkins that wanted to eat her brains. Her tears seemed to grieve the kind-hearted Munchkins, for they immediately took out their handkerchiefs and began to weep also. As for the little old woman, she took off her cap and balanced the point on the end of her nose, while she counted "One, two, three" in a solemn voice. At once the cap changed to a slate, on which was written in big, white chalk marks:

"LET DOROTHY GO TO THE CITY OF EMERALDS"

The little old woman took the slate from her nose, and having read the words on it, asked, "Is your name Dorothy, my dear?"

"Yes," answered the child, looking up and drying her tears.

"Then you must go to the City of Emeralds. Perhaps Oz will help you."

"Where is this city?" asked Dorothy.

"It is exactly in the center of the country, and is ruled by Oz, the Great Wizard I told you of."

"Is he a good man?" inquired the girl anxiously.

"He is a good Wizard. Whether he is a man or not I cannot tell, for I have never seen him."

"How can I get there?" asked Dorothy.

"You must walk. It is a long journey, through a country that is sometimes pleasant and sometimes dark and terrible. However, I will use all the magic arts I know of to keep you from harm."

"Then I'm pretty much done for."

"I am stronger than you think."

"Just not strong enough to stop the brain-eating creatures."

"We're called Munchkins," said one of the little men beside her. He had a fresh scar above his eye. "I thought we covered this already."

"We did," the Witch said calmly. "Now, Dorothy, you must trust me that I can help you on your journey, for not everything in this land is under the control of witches."

"Most of it is, though," said the scarred Munchkin.

"Ain't that the truth," added one of his friends.

"Hush, you two," said the old woman.

"Won't you go with me?" pleaded the girl, who had begun to look upon the little old woman as her only friend.

"No, I cannot do that," the Witch replied, "but I will give you my kiss, and no one will dare injure a person who has been kissed by the Witch of the North."

She came close to Dorothy and kissed her gently on the forehead. Where her lips touched the girl they left a round, shining mark, as Dorothy found out soon after.

"The road to the City of Emeralds is paved with yellow brick," said the Witch, "so you cannot miss it. When you get to Oz do not be afraid of him, but tell your story and ask him to help you. And if you would be so kind, please ask him to help us as well, for only the great Oz will know how to end our plague of undead."

"I promise I will," replied Dorothy.

The Munchkins bowed low to her and wished her a pleasant journey, after which they walked away through the trees, their tiny guns cocked and ready to fire at anything unnatural. The Witch gave Dorothy a friendly little nod, whirled around on her left heel three times, and straightway disappeared, much to the surprise of little Toto, who barked after her loudly enough when she had gone, because he had been afraid even to growl while everyone stood by. But Dorothy, knowing her to be a witch, had expected her to disappear in just that way, and was not surprised in the least. It seemed to be the one power she was good at.

3

How Dorothy Saved
the Scarecrow

W HEN DOROTHY WAS left alone she began to feel hungry. So she went to the cupboard of her house and cut herself some bread, which she spread with butter. She gave some to Toto, and taking a pail from the shelf she carried it down to the little brook and filled it with clear, sparkling water. Toto ran over to the trees and began to bark at the birds sitting there. Dorothy went to get him, and saw such delicious fruit hanging from the branches that she gathered some of it, finding it just what she wanted to help out her breakfast.

Then she went back to the house, and having helped herself and Toto to a good drink of the cool, clear water, she set about making ready for the journey to the City of Emeralds.

Dorothy had only one other dress, but that happened to be clean and was hanging on a peg beside her bed. It was gingham, with checks of white and blue; and although the blue was somewhat faded with many washings, it was still a pretty frock. The girl washed herself carefully, dressed herself in the clean gingham, and tied her pink sunbonnet on her head. She took a little basket and filled it with bread from the cupboard, laying a white cloth over the top. Then she looked down at her feet and noticed how old and worn her shoes were.

"They surely will never do for a long journey, Toto," she said. And Toto looked up into her face with his little black eyes and wagged his tail to show he knew what she meant.

At that moment Dorothy saw lying on the table the silver shoes that had belonged to the Witch of the East. They were now part ruby-colored thanks to all the dried blood from the battle.

"I wonder if they will fit me," she said to Toto. "They would be just the thing to take a long walk in, for they could not wear out."

She took off her old leather shoes and tried on the silver

bloodstained ones, which fitted her as well as if they had been made for her.

Finally she picked up her basket.

"Come along, Toto," she said. "We will go to the Emerald City and ask the Great Oz how to get back to Kansas and how to save the Munchkins."

She closed the door, locked it, and put the key carefully in the pocket of her dress. And so, with Toto trotting along soberly behind her, she started on her journey.

There were several roads nearby, but it did not take her long to find the one paved with yellow bricks. Within a short time she was walking briskly toward the Emerald City, her silver shoes tinkling merrily on the hard, yellow road-bed. The sun shone bright and the birds sang sweetly, and Dorothy did not feel nearly so bad as you might think a little girl would who had been suddenly whisked away from her own country and set down in the midst of a strange land with walking dead creatures . . . er . . . people.

She was surprised, as she walked along, to see how pretty the country was about her. There were neat fences at the sides of the road, painted a dainty blue color, and beyond them were fields of grain and vegetables in abundance. Evidently the Munchkins were good farmers and able to raise large crops. Once in a while she would pass a house, its windows boarded up and the door with little gun holes cut into it. The people came out to look at her and bow low as she went by; for everyone knew she had been the means of destroying the Wicked Witch and would help them get rid of their curse. The houses of the Munchkins were odd-looking dwellings, for each was round, with a big dome for a roof. All were painted blue, for in this country of the East blue was the favorite color. All of them were reinforced with tree trunks and sharp gardening tools in preparation for some kind of battle. Even the gardening tools had been painted blue.

Toward evening, when Dorothy was tired with her long walk and began to wonder where she should pass the night, she came to a house rather larger than the rest. On the green lawn before it many men and women were dancing. Five little fiddlers played as loudly as possible, and the people were laughing and singing, while a big table near by was loaded with delicious fruits and nuts, pies and cakes, and many other good things to eat. On another table to the side lay a collection of tiny rifles. At this table sat more little men, all with stern countenances, for they were watching the lands around them for the undead.

The people greeted Dorothy kindly, and invited her to supper and to pass the night with them; for this was the home of one of the richest Munchkins in the land, and his friends were gathered with him to celebrate the death of the Wicked Witch.

Dorothy ate a hearty supper and was waited upon by the rich Munchkin himself, whose name was Boq. Then she sat upon a settee and watched the people dance.

When Boq saw her bloodied, silver shoes he said, "You must be a great sorceress."

"Why?" asked the girl.

"Because you wear silver shoes and have killed the Wicked Witch. Besides, you have white in your frock, and only witches and sorceresses wear white."

"My dress is blue and white checked, and has a spot of blood here," said Dorothy, smoothing out the wrinkles in it and trying to smear the blood away with some saliva.

"It is kind of you to wear that," said Boq. "Blue is the color of the Munchkins, and white is the witch color. So we know you are a friendly witch."

Dorothy did not know what to say to this, for all the people seemed to think her a witch, and she knew very well she was only an ordinary little girl who had come by the chance of a cyclone into a strange land of little people and the walking dead.

When she had tired watching the dancing, Boq led her into the house, where he gave her a room with a pretty bed in it. The sheets were made of blue cloth, and even the boards nailed up over the windows were as bright blue as a midday sky. Before she fell asleep, Boq knocked and asked to enter. "Come in," said Dorothy. Boq entered carrying one of the tiny rifles Dorothy had seen on the table outside. He handed it to her with great care.

"This is my most accurate shooter," he said with a wide smile. "Its bullets have been enchanted by the Witch of the North. I want you to have it to aid you on your quest."

"Thank you," said Dorothy, cradling the gun, which was bright blue with patches of silver. She showed it to Toto and the little dog barked his approval. "However, I do not know how to shoot."

"That is no bother," said Boq, "for all you do is squeeze the trigger and the magical gun will do the rest."

Dorothy was so happy to have a magical weapon to protect her that she gave Boq a little kiss on the cheek. "Thank you so much for helping me. But I am so very tired now that I must rest for a while."

Dorothy slept soundly in the comfortable blue bed till morning, with Toto curled up on the blue rug beside her. The magical blue rifle leaned against the wall nearby.

She ate a hearty breakfast, and watched a wee Munchkin baby, who played with Toto and pulled his tail and crowed and laughed in a way that greatly amused Dorothy. Toto was a fine curiosity to all the people, for they had never seen a dog before.

"How far is it to the Emerald City?" the girl asked.

"I do not know," answered Boq gravely, "for I have never been there. It is better for people to keep away from Oz, unless they have business with him. But it is a long way to the Emerald City, and it will take you many days. The country here is rich and pleasant, but you must pass through rough and dangerous places full of monsters and other creatures both alive and dead before you reach the end of your journey."

"Other creatures?" Dorothy asked. "Alive and dead?"

"Oh yes, the Wicked Witch has not just plagued us Munchkins, but the entire land. So much of what has died in the years past has come back to roam the lands in search of fresh brains."

This worried Dorothy a little, but she felt safer with Boq's gift, and knew that only the Great Oz could help her get to Kansas again, and perhaps reverse the Wicked Witch's curse, so she bravely resolved not to turn back.

She bade her friends good-bye, and again started along the road of yellow brick. When she had gone several miles she thought she would stop to rest, and so climbed to the top of the fence beside the road and sat down. There was a great cornfield beyond the fence, and not far away she saw a Scarecrow, placed high on a pole to keep the birds from the ripe corn.

Dorothy leaned her chin upon her hand and gazed thoughtfully at the Scarecrow. Its head was a small sack stuffed with straw, with eyes, nose, and mouth painted on it to represent a face. An old, pointed blue hat that had belonged to some Munchkin, was perched on his head, and the rest of the figure was a blue suit of clothes, worn and faded, which had also been stuffed with straw. On the feet were some old boots with blue tops, such as every man wore in this country, and the figure was raised above the stalks of corn by means of the pole stuck up its back.

While Dorothy was looking earnestly into the queer, painted face of the Scarecrow, she was surprised to see one of the eyes slowly wink at her. She thought she must have been mistaken at first, for none of the scarecrows in Kansas ever wink; but presently the figure nodded its head to her in a friendly way. Then she climbed down from the fence and walked up to it, while Toto ran around the pole and barked.

"Good day," said the Scarecrow, in a rather husky voice.

"Did you speak?" asked the girl, in wonder.

"Certainly," answered the Scarecrow. "How do you do?"

"I'm pretty well, thank you," replied Dorothy politely. "How do you do?"

"I'm not feeling well," said the Scarecrow, with a smile, "for it is very tedious being perched up here night and day to scare away crows."

"Can't you get down?" asked Dorothy.

"No, for this pole is stuck up my back. If you will please take away the pole I shall be greatly obliged to you."

Dorothy reached up both arms and lifted the figure off the pole, for, being stuffed with straw, it was quite light.

"Thank you very much," said the Scarecrow, when he had been set down on the ground. "I feel like a new man."

Dorothy was puzzled at this, for it sounded queer to hear a stuffed man speak, and to see him bow and walk along beside her.

"I should look behind you if I were you," said the Scarecrow.

Dorothy turned just in time to see a handful of little men with faces as gray as slab shuffling toward her through the cornfield. "Oh no," she cried. "It's more of those horrible dead creatures."

"Yes," said the Scarecrow, who was now eyeing four ratty crows flying down from the trees near the road. The crows were also dead, with bones sticking out of their feathers and ghastly hollow eye sockets. "It seems the Wicked Witch's minions have followed you."

"Whatever shall we do," cried Dorothy.

"I was hoping your gun might help us out."

"Oh, right," said Dorothy who had forgotten she was holding the gun. She raised the weapon, terrified by the notion she was going to shoot something, and pulled the trigger. There was a loud bang and the head of the undead Munchkin closest to her exploded in a starburst of wet blue goo.

"Good shot!" exclaimed the Scarecrow. "But look out, there are more!"

Before she could fire again, the remaining monsters lurched forward and grabbed her arms and legs. She screamed, horrified of the hungry rotting corpses, and struggled to get herself free. Meanwhile the Scarecrow had been set upon by the cadaverous crows, which stabbed their beaks into his head and began pulling all of the straw out.

"Fire again!" shouted the Scarecrow. He was now rolling on the ground, a crow in each hand. He squeezed them tightly until their bird blood gushed through his fingers. "Fire!"

Toto jumped at the gray creature trying to bite Dorothy's arm, got a mouthful of the creature's shirt and yanked furiously until the creature let go. Dorothy was able to swing the gun around now and fired it wildly. There was an even louder bang this time, and she felt something whiz by her face. Just as she managed to get the rest of her limbs free from her attackers, she saw each of the undead Munchkins' heads burst open like rotten tomatoes thrown against a rock wall. In an instant they all fell motionless around her.

"Was that just one bullet?"

The Scarecrow, now holding all of the dead, crushed crows in his hand, nodded. "It appears you have magic bullets, child. Your one shot tore through all of their heads, one after the other." The Scarecrow proceeded to rip the heads off all of the bloody crows and throw them to the ground. He wiped the birds' blood off on his chest.

Dorothy helped him stuff the straw back in his head, and he in turn helped her wash some of the thick blood off of her face. "Aunt Em would be so angry if she saw how dirty I was," Dorothy said.

"Who are you?" asked the Scarecrow. "And where are you going?"

"My name is Dorothy," said the girl, "and I am going to the Emerald City, to ask the Great Oz to send me back to Kansas.

"Where is the Emerald City?" he inquired. "And who is Oz?"

"Why, don't you know?" she returned, in surprise.

"No, indeed. I don't know anything. You see, I am stuffed, so I have no brains at all," he answered sadly.

"Oh," said Dorothy, "I'm awfully sorry for you. That must explain why all those dead Munchkins only came after me."

"Do you think," he asked, "if I go to the Emerald City with you, that Oz would give me some brains?"

"I cannot tell," she returned, "but you may come with me, if you like. If Oz will not give you any brains you will be no worse off than you are now."

"That is true," said the Scarecrow. "You see," he continued confidentially, "I don't mind my legs and arms and body being stuffed, because I cannot get hurt. If anyone treads on my toes or sticks a pin into me, it doesn't matter, for I can't feel it. The crows only attack to try and tear me apart so I cannot move anymore. They are quite mean in that fashion. But I do not want people to call me a fool, and if my head stays stuffed with straw instead of with brains, as yours is, how am I ever to know anything?"

"I understand how you feel," said the little girl, who was truly sorry for him. "If you will come with me I'll ask Oz to do all he can for you. Although if he gives you some brains, you will have to worry about these creatures wanting to eat them."

"I would rather be wanted than unwanted."

"Then you shall come with me and together we will seek out the Great Oz."

"Thank you," he answered gratefully.

They walked back to the road. Dorothy helped him over the fence, and they started along the path of yellow brick for the Emerald City.

Toto did not like this addition to the party at first. He smelled around the stuffed man as if he suspected there might be a nest of rats in the straw, and he often growled in an unfriendly way at the Scarecrow.

"Don't mind Toto," said Dorothy to her new friend. "He never bites."

"Oh, I'm not afraid," replied the Scarecrow. "He can't hurt the straw. Besides, he looks like he will soon be more interested in hurting you than me."

Dorothy was confused by this, but when she picked up Toto she noticed a small bite on his tail. "Oh no, one of those creature must have bit him."

"Indeed they did, which means he will soon have a craving for brains, for that is how the evil magic works."

"How horrible. Toto is my best friend. I do not want him to turn into one of those monsters."

"They we must hurry to Oz," said the Scarecrow, "for only he might be able to save the little fella. Do let me carry that basket for you. I shall not mind it, for I can't get tired. I'll tell you a secret," he continued, as he walked along. "There is only one thing in the world I am afraid of."

"What is that?" asked Dorothy; "a brain-eater?"

"No," answered the Scarecrow; "a brain-eater carrying a lighted match."

4

The Road Through
the Undead Forest

AFTER A FEW hours the road began to be rough, and the walking grew so difficult that the Scarecrow often stumbled over the yellow bricks, which were here very uneven. Sometimes, indeed, they were broken or missing altogether, leaving holes that Toto jumped across and Dorothy walked around. As for the Scarecrow, having no brains, he walked straight ahead, and so stepped into the holes and fell at full length on the hard bricks. It never hurt him, however, and Dorothy would pick him up and set him upon his feet again, while he joined her in laughing merrily at his own mishap.

The farms were not nearly so well cared for here as they were farther back. There were fewer houses and fewer fruit trees, and the farther they went the more dismal and lonesome the country became. There were signs of attack from the undead Munchkins. Patches of blood and even severed limbs dotted the landscape. Dorothy held her fingers over her nose as they passed for the stench was worse than her Uncle's pig pens on a hot summer day.

At noon they sat down by the roadside, near a little brook, and Dorothy opened her basket and got out some bread. She offered a piece to the Scarecrow, but he refused.

"I am never hungry," he said, "and it is a lucky thing I am not, for my mouth is only painted, and if I should cut a hole in it so I could eat, the straw I am stuffed with would come out, and that would spoil the shape of my head."

Dorothy saw at once that this was true, so she only nodded and went on eating her bread. She pet Toto, who was looking more tired now. The wound on his tail appeared to be getting worse.

"Tell me something about yourself and the country you came from," said the Scarecrow, when she had finished her dinner. So she told him all about Kansas, and how gray everything was there, and how the cyclone had carried her to this queer Land of Oz.

The Scarecrow listened carefully, and said, "I cannot understand why you should wish to leave this beautiful country and go back to the dry, gray place you call Kansas."

"That is because you have no brains" answered the girl. "No matter how dreary and gray our homes are, we people of flesh and blood would rather live there than in any other country, be it ever so beautiful. There is no place like home."

The Scarecrow sighed. "Of course I cannot understand it," he said. "If your heads were stuffed with straw, like mine, you would probably all live in the beautiful places, and then Kansas would have no people at all. It is fortunate for Kansas that you have brains."

"Yes, unfortunately it's not so lucky in your land to have brains, for they will be eaten by the Witch's plague. But won't you tell me a story, while we are resting?" asked the child.

The Scarecrow looked at her reproachfully, and answered: "My life has been so short that I really know nothing whatever. I was only made day before yesterday. What happened in the world before that time is all unknown to me. Luckily, when the farmer made my head, one of the first things he did was to paint my ears, so that I heard what was going on. There was another Munchkin with him, and the first thing I heard was the farmer saying, 'How do you like those ears?'

"'They aren't straight,' answered the other.

"'Never mind,' said the farmer. 'They are ears just the same,' which was true enough.

"'Now I'll make the eyes,' said the farmer. So he painted my right eye, and as soon as it was finished I found myself looking at him and at everything around me with a great deal of curiosity, for this was my first glimpse of the world.

"'That's a rather pretty eye,' remarked the Munchkin who was watching the farmer. 'Blue paint is just the color for eyes.'

"'I think I'll make the other a little bigger,' said the farmer. And when the second eye was done I could see much better than before. Then he made my nose and my mouth. But I did not speak, because at that time I didn't know what a mouth was for. I had the fun of watching them make my body and my arms and legs; and when they fastened on my head, at last, I felt very proud, for I thought I was just as good a man as anyone.

"'This fellow will scare the crows fast enough,' said the farmer. 'He looks just like a man.'

"'Why, he is a man,' said the other, and I quite agreed with him. The farmer carried me under his arm to the cornfield, and set me up on a tall stick, where you found me. He and his friend were soon after killed by the undead. The creatures came out of the cornfields and attacked without warning. I tried to get down and save my maker and his friend, but my feet would not touch the ground, and I was forced to stay on that pole as the fight unfolded around me. As I watched, the farmer and his friend put up a good fight, taking off several of the creatures' heads with their scythes, but eventually the evil little undead Munchkins sank their teeth into the farmer's head and ate out his eyeballs. I would have drawn some on him as he did to me, but alas I still could not move. Soon after the farmer's friend was wrestled to the ground and the monsters tore his face off and ate his brains through his eye sockets. For the rest of the day they ate him until he was nothing more than a skeleton."

"And what of the farmer?" asked Dorothy.

"Soon he woke up, moaning for brains, and joined the other undead Munchkins, for they did not eat enough of him to finish him off for good. I could see his ribs and even his heart, which flapped about in a hole in his chest, but it did not stop him from moving. The next night the farmer returned from the cornfield and walked into his house. I could see through the tiny bedroom window as he bit his wife, who was sleeping in their little blue bed, and ate her brains. Then even she rose from the dead and together they walked off into the corn. They would have continued walking and eating people for days to come had you not shot them with your magic bullet earlier."

Dorothy rubbed Toto's little head, worried more than ever about him turning into such an evil monster. The little dog wagged his tail, but Dorothy could see he was feeling quite awful and sick.

"Then I was alone," the Scarecrow continued. "It was a lonely life to lead, for I had nothing to think of, having been made such a little while before. Many crows and other birds flew into the cornfield, but as soon as they saw me they flew away again, thinking I was a Munchkin; and this pleased me and made me feel that I was quite an important person. By and by an old crow flew near me, and after looking at me carefully he perched upon my shoulder and said:

"'I wonder if that farmer thought to fool me in this clumsy manner. Any crow of sense could see that you are only stuffed with straw.' Then he hopped down at my feet and ate all the corn he wanted. The other birds, seeing he was not harmed by me, came to eat the corn too, so in a short time there was a great flock of them about me.

"In time the crows came back dead. I do not know if the walking dead Munchkins bit them or if these undead crows died naturally, but either way they seemed to want to taunt me. They would peck at my head and laugh and cry, 'No brains, no brains.' For I assume having no need of corn anymore they were just bored and wanted to be mean.

"I felt sad at this, for it showed I was not such a good Scarecrow after all; but a normal crow comforted me, saying, 'If you only had brains in your head you would at least be put out of your misery. Brains are the only things that matter in this part of the country.'

"After the crows had gone I thought this over, and decided I would try hard to get some brains. By good luck you came along and pulled me off the stake, and from what you say I am sure the Great Oz will give me brains as soon as we get to the Emerald City."

"I hope so," said Dorothy earnestly, "since you seem anxious to have them."

"Oh, yes; I am anxious," returned the Scarecrow. "It is such an uncomfortable feeling to know one is both foolish and unwanted."

"Well," said the girl, "let us go." And she handed the basket to the Scarecrow.

There were no fences at all by the roadside now, and the land was rough and untilled. Toward evening they came to a great forest, where the trees grew so big and close together that their branches met over the road of yellow brick. It was almost dark under the trees, for the branches shut out the daylight; but the travelers did not stop, and went on into the forest.

"If this road goes in, it must come out," said the Scarecrow, "and as the Emerald City is at the other end of the road, we must go wherever it leads us."

"Anyone would know that," said Dorothy.

"Certainly; that is why I know it," returned the Scarecrow. "If it required brains to figure it out, I never should have said it."

After an hour or so the light faded away, and they found themselves stumbling along in the darkness. Dorothy could not see at all, but Toto could, for some dogs see very well in the dark; and the Scarecrow declared he could see as well as by day. So she took hold of his arm and managed to get along fairly well.

But the deeper they went the darker it became, and Dorothy was worried because the undead could be hiding anywhere. She clutched her magic gun closer to her chest, just in case. Every so often they would hear moans coming from the forest around them. "Those are the hungry undead," warned the Scarecrow, although he did not sound afraid because he knew the undead did not want him.

At one point, as the road wound to the left, a figure stood in the dark shadows ahead of them. It walked toward them slowly, with its arms outstretched. "Braiiins," it moaned, in what almost sounded like a pretty girl's voice.

"Is that one of the creatures?" Dorothy asked, for she could not see well enough in the dark.

"It is indeed," answered the Scarecrow. "You should shoot it before it gets you."

"But I can barely see."

"Ah yes, but you are forgetting your magical gun."

"How silly of me," Dorothy answered. "It is a good thing you thought of it."

She raised the gun and pointed it in the direction of the approaching undead Munchkin. Though she was wildly off target, she squeezed the trigger with confidence. The bullet zipped around many of the trees surrounding them, and she heard the wet sounds of it passing through the heads of the undead hiding deep among the trees. She heard several bodies fall to the leafy forest floor even though she could not see them. A minute later the bullet came back out of the woods and cleaved the shambling figure's head in two. Its body slumped to the bricks and lay still.

"Nice shot," said the Scarecrow. They walked over to the body and Dorothy could now see it was in fact a girl, a girl Munchkin wearing what had once been a pretty blue dress. But now the girl's flesh had rotted away and her eyes were missing.

"If you see any house, or any place where we can pass the night," Dorothy said, "you must tell me; for it is very uncomfortable walking in the dark with all of these creatures."

Soon after the Scarecrow stopped.

"I see a little cottage at the right of us," he said, "built of logs and branches. Shall we go there?"

"Yes, indeed," answered the child. "I am all tired out."

So the Scarecrow led her through the trees until they reached the cottage, and Dorothy entered and found a bed of dried leaves in one corner. She lay down at once, and with Toto beside her soon fell into a sound sleep. The Scarecrow, who was never tired, stood up in another corner and waited patiently until morning came.

5

The Rescue of the Tin Woodman

When Dorothy awoke the sun was shining through the trees and Toto had long been out chasing birds around him and squirrels. His mouth was covered in blood and his eyes were looking glazed. She sat up and looked around her. Scarecrow, still standing patiently in his corner, was waiting for her.

"We must go and search for water," she said to him.

"Why do you want water?" he asked.

"To wash my face clean after the dust of the road, and to drink, so the dry bread will not stick in my throat. Also so it might make Toto feel better."

"It must be inconvenient to be made of flesh," said the Scarecrow thoughtfully, "for you must sleep, and eat and drink. However, you have brains, and it is worth a lot of bother to be able to think and be wanted."

They left the cottage and walked through the trees until they found a little spring of clear water, where Dorothy drank and bathed and ate her breakfast. She saw there was not much bread left in the basket, and the girl was thankful the Scarecrow did not have to eat anything, for there was scarcely enough for herself and Toto for the day, although Toto looked full from eating the squirrels. She urged him to drink but he did not seem interested.

When she had finished her meal, and was about to go back to the road of yellow brick, she was startled to hear a deep groan near by.

"What was that?" she asked timidly. "I hope it's not more of those dreadful dead Munchkins."

"I cannot imagine," replied the Scarecrow; "but we can go and see."

Just then another groan reached their ears, and the sound seemed to come from behind them. They turned and walked through the forest a few steps, when Dorothy discovered something shining in a ray of sunshine that fell between the trees. She ran to the place and then stopped short, with a little cry of surprise.

One of the big trees had been partly chopped through, and standing beside it, with an uplifted axe in his hands, was a man made entirely of tin. His head and arms and legs were jointed upon his body, but he stood perfectly motionless, as if he could not stir at all.

Dorothy looked at him in amazement, and so did the Scarecrow, while Toto barked sharply and made a snap at the tin legs, which hurt his teeth.

"Did you groan?" asked Dorothy.

"Yes," answered the tin man, "I did. I've been groaning for more than a year, and no one has ever come to help me."

Dorothy noticed many teeth marks on his tin head and asked, "Who has been biting you?"

"Oh, that. The undead come by regularly and try to get at my brain," said the Tin Woodman, "but my head is too strong for them so eventually they give up and leave. It is the only company I've had in a year."

"What can I do for you?" she inquired softly, for she was moved by the sad voice in which the man spoke.

"Get an oil-can and oil my joints," he answered. "They are rusted so badly that I cannot move them at all; if I am well oiled I shall soon be all right again. You will find an oil-can on a shelf in my cottage."

Dorothy at once ran back to the cottage and found the oil-can, and then she returned and asked anxiously, "Where are your joints?"

"Oil my neck, first," replied the Tin Woodman. So she oiled it, and as it was quite badly rusted the Scarecrow took hold of the tin head and moved it gently from side to side until it worked freely, and then the man could turn it himself.

"Now oil the joints in my arms," he said. And Dorothy oiled them and the Scarecrow bent them carefully until they were quite free from rust and as good as new.

The Tin Woodman gave a sigh of satisfaction and lowered his axe, which he leaned against the tree.

"This is a great comfort," he said. "I have been holding that axe in the air ever since I rusted, and I'm glad to be able to put it down at last. Now, if you will oil the joints of my legs, I shall be all right once more."

So they oiled his legs until he could move them freely; and he thanked them again and again for his release, for he seemed a very polite creature, and very grateful.

"I might have stood there always, tolerating the ugly dead Munchkins biting me, if you had not come along," he said; "so you have certainly saved my life. How did you happen to be here?"

"We are on our way to the Emerald City to see the Great Oz," she answered, "and we stopped at your cottage to pass the night."

"Why do you wish to see Oz?" he asked.

"I want him to send me back to Kansas, the Scarecrow wants him to put a few brains into his head, and the Witch of the North asked us to have him end the horrible plague of the undead," she replied.

The Tin Woodman appeared to think deeply for a moment. Then he said: "Do you suppose Oz could give me a heart?"

"Why, I guess so," Dorothy answered. "It would be as easy as to give the Scarecrow brains."

"True," the Tin Woodman returned. "So, if you will allow me to join your party, I will also go to the Emerald City and ask Oz to help me."

"Come along," said the Scarecrow heartily, and Dorothy added that she would be pleased to have his company. So the Tin Woodman shouldered his axe and they all passed through the forest until they came to the road that was paved with yellow brick.

The Tin Woodman had asked Dorothy to put the oil-can in her basket. "For," he said, "if I should get caught in the rain, and rust again, I would need the oil-can badly."

It was a bit of good luck to have their new comrade join the party, for soon after they had begun their journey again they came to a place where the trees and branches grew so thick over the road that the travelers could not pass. But the Tin Woodman set to work with his axe and chopped so well that soon he cleared a passage for the entire party.

Dorothy was thinking so earnestly as they walked along that she did not notice when the Scarecrow stumbled into a hole and rolled over to the side of the road. Indeed he was obliged to call to her to help him up again.

"Why didn't you walk around the hole?" asked the Tin Woodman.

"I don't know enough," replied the Scarecrow cheerfully. "My head is stuffed with straw, you know, and that is why I am going to Oz to ask him for some brains."

"Oh, I see," said the Tin Woodman. "But, after all, brains are not the best things in the world. They attract all of these hungry, rotted Munchkins."

"Have you any brains?" inquired the Scarecrow.

"No, my head is quite empty," answered the Woodman. But once I had brains, and the dead can still sense them, I suppose. I had a heart also; so, having tried them both, I should much rather have a heart."

"And why is that?" asked the Scarecrow.

"I will tell you my story, and then you will know."

So, while they were walking through the forest, the Tin Woodman told the following story: "I was born the son of a woodman who chopped down trees in the forest and sold the wood for a living. When I grew up, I too became a woodchopper, and after my father died I took care of my old mother as long as she lived. Then I made up my mind that instead of living alone I would marry, so that I might not become lonely.

"There was one of the Munchkin girls who was so beautiful that I soon grew to love her with all my heart. She, on her part, promised to marry me as soon as I could earn enough money to build a better house for her; so I set to work harder than ever. But the girl lived with an old woman who did not want her to marry anyone, for she was so lazy she wished the girl to remain with her and do the cooking and the housework. So the old woman went to the Wicked Witch of the East, and promised her two sheep and a cow if she would prevent the marriage. Thereupon the Wicked Witch enchanted my axe, and when I was chopping away at a couple of rotted, hungry dead Munchkins, the axe slipped all at once and cut off my left leg.

"This at first seemed a great misfortune, for I knew a one-legged man could not do very well as a protector. So I went to a tinsmith and had him make me a new leg out of tin. The leg worked very well, once I was used to it. But my action angered the Wicked Witch of the East, for she had promised the old woman I should not marry the pretty Munchkin girl. Days later, when I was beset upon by more ugly undead, my axe slipped and cut off my right leg. Again I went to the tinsmith, and again he made me a leg out of tin. After this the enchanted axe cut off my arms, one after the other; but, nothing daunted, I had them replaced with tin ones. The Wicked Witch then made the axe slip and cut off my head, and at first I thought that was the end of me. But the tinsmith happened to come along, and he made me a new head out of tin.

"I thought I had beaten the Wicked Witch then, and I worked harder than ever; but I little knew how cruel my enemy could be. She thought of a new way to kill my love for the beautiful Munchkin maiden, and made my axe slip again, so that it cut right through my body, splitting me into two halves. Once more the tinsmith came to my help and made me a body of tin, fastening my tin arms and legs and head to it, by means of joints, so that I could move around as well as ever. But, alas! I had now no heart, so that I lost all my love for the Munchkin girl, and did not care whether I married her or not. Soon after it did not matter anyway, for the girl I loved was ambushed by the brain-eaters while collecting flowers one day, and they ate off her skin. Now she walks around in the forest moaning for brains."

Dorothy was suddenly sure she must have killed the tin man's former girlfriend the previous night, but did not say this, for she could tell it would make him sad.

The Tin Woodman continued his story: "My body shone so brightly in the sun that I felt very proud of it and it did not matter now if my axe slipped, for it could not cut me. There was only one danger—that my joints would rust; but I kept an oil-can in my cottage and took care to oil myself whenever I needed it. However, there came a day when I forgot to do this, and was suddenly attacked by more of those miserable, brain-hungry things. As I fought them back, chopping their heads off and splitting their little bodies in two so they could no longer eat anyone, I realized I was caught in a rainstorm. Before I could retreat to the safety of my cottage, my joints had rusted, and I was left to stand in the woods until you came to help me. It was a terrible thing to undergo, but during the year I stood there, letting the little Munchkin creatures gnaw at my tin head, trying to explain to them that my brains were no longer inside, I had time to think that the greatest loss I had known was the loss of my heart. While I was in love I was the happiest man on earth; but no one can love who has not a heart, and so I am resolved to ask Oz to give me one. If he does, and if he can turn the undead back to the living, then I will go back to the Munchkin maiden and marry her."

Both Dorothy and the Scarecrow shared a look but said nothing of the girl in the woods, for this man was wielding an axe after all. But now they knew why he was so anxious to get a new heart. Dorothy was skeptical, however, that Oz could turn the undead back to the living, even if she hadn't killed the Tin Woodman's old girlfriend in the woods.

"All the same," said the Scarecrow, "I shall ask for brains instead of a heart; for a fool would not know what to do with a heart if he had one."

"I shall take the heart," returned the Tin Woodman; "for brains do not make one happy, they merely attract the flesh-eaters, and happiness is the best thing in the world."

Dorothy did not say anything, for she was puzzled to know which of her two friends was right, and was more concerned about Toto, whose fur seemed to be turning grayer. She decided if she could only save her sick little friend, who had not yet fully turned into one of the undead, and get back to Kansas and Aunt Em, it did not matter so much whether the Woodman had no brains and the Scarecrow no heart, or each got what he wanted.

What worried her most was that the bread was nearly gone, and another meal for herself would empty the basket. To be sure neither the Woodman nor the Scarecrow ever ate anything, but she was not made of tin nor straw, and could not live unless she was fed. And the last thing she wanted to eat was someone's brains.

6
The Cowardly Lion

ALL THIS TIME Dorothy and her companions had been walking through the thick woods. The road was still paved with yellow brick, but these were much covered by dried branches and dead leaves from the trees, and the walking was not at all good. Several times they saw dead bodies on the road. Most were mere skeletons, and Toto sniffed their bones and licked any remaining blood off of them. Every time he did that, Dorothy felt sick inside. These they stepped over carefully, for no one knew if they would rise up or not.

There were few birds in this part of the forest, for birds love the open country where there is plenty of sunshine. But now and then there came a deep growl from some wild animal hidden among the trees. These sounds made the little girl's heart beat fast, for she did not know what made them; but Toto knew, and he walked close to Dorothy's side, and did not even bark in return.

"How long will it be," the child asked of the Tin Woodman, "before we are out of the forest?"

"I cannot tell," was the answer, "for I have never been to the Emerald City. But my father went there once, when I was a boy, and he said it was a long journey through a dangerous country, although nearer to the city where Oz dwells the country is beautiful. But I am not afraid so long as I have my oil-can, and nothing can hurt the Scarecrow, while you bear upon your forehead the mark of the Good Witch's kiss, and that will protect you from harm."

"But Toto!" said the girl anxiously. "What will protect him?"

"We must protect him ourselves if he is in danger," replied the Tin Woodman.

"I don't think it will be long before he turns," said the Scarecrow, "so we might not need to worry. Though I suppose the living monsters in this land will still want to eat him."

Just as he spoke there came from the forest a terrible roar, and the next moment a great Lion bounded into the road. With one blow of his paw he sent the Scarecrow spinning over and over to the edge of the road, and then he struck at the Tin Woodman with his sharp claws. But, to the Lion's surprise, he could make no impression on the tin, although the Woodman fell over in the road and lay still.

Little Toto, now that he had an enemy to face, ran barking toward the Lion, and the great beast had opened his mouth to bite the dog, when Dorothy, fearing Toto would be killed, and heedless of danger, rushed forward and slapped the Lion upon his nose as hard as she could with her magical gun, while she cried out:

"Don't you dare to bite Toto! You ought to be ashamed of yourself, a big beast like you, to bite a poor little dog!"

"I didn't bite him," said the Lion, as he rubbed his nose with his paw where Dorothy had hit it. "Besides, it looks like he's already been bitten by something else."

"That may be, but you tried to bite him too," she retorted. "You are nothing but a big coward."

"I know it," said the Lion, hanging his head in shame. "I've always known it. But how can I help it?"

"I don't know, I'm sure. To think of your striking a stuffed man, like the poor Scarecrow!"

"Is he stuffed?" asked the Lion in surprise, as he watched her pick up the Scarecrow and set him upon his feet, while she patted him into shape again. "He looked like one of those awful men that are always eating people's brains."

"He does not! He looks like a simple stuffed man," replied Dorothy, who was still angry.

"So then he is stuffed. That's why he went over so easily," remarked the Lion. "It astonished me to see him whirl around so. Is the other one stuffed also?"

"No," said Dorothy, "he's made of tin." And she helped the Woodman up again.

"That's why he nearly blunted my claws," said the Lion. "When they scratched against the tin it made a cold shiver run down my back. What is that little animal you are so tender of?"

"He is my dog, Toto," answered Dorothy.

"Is he made of tin, or stuffed?" asked the Lion.

"Neither. He's a—a—a meat dog," said the girl.

"Oh! Does he eat brains?"

"Of course not!"

"At least not yet," added the Scarecrow.

"Not helping," Dorothy snapped.

"He's a curious animal and seems remarkably small, now that I look at him," continued the Lion. "No one would think of biting such a little thing, except a coward or a monster."

"What makes you a coward?" asked Dorothy, looking at the great beast in wonder, for he was as big as a small horse.

"It's a mystery," replied the Lion. "I suppose I was born that way. All the other animals in the forest naturally expect me to be brave, for the Lion is everywhere thought to be the King of Beasts. I learned that if I roared very loudly every living thing was frightened and got out of my way. Whenever I've met a man I've been awfully scared; but I just roared at him, and he has always run away as fast as he could go. If the elephants and the tigers and the bears had ever tried to fight me, I should have run myself—I'm such a coward; but just as soon as they hear me roar they all try to get away from me, and of course I let them go. The only ones who do not run are the ones hungry for brains, and I didn't see the Scarecrow running."

"That's because I don't have any brains and therefore am never afraid," said the Scarecrow. "But The King of Beasts shouldn't be a coward."

"I know it," returned the Lion, wiping a tear from his eye with the tip of his tail. "It is my great sorrow, and makes my life very unhappy. But whenever there is danger, my heart begins to beat fast."

"Perhaps you have heart disease," said the Tin Woodman.

"It may be," said the Lion.

"If you have," continued the Tin Woodman, "you ought to be glad, for it proves you have a heart. For my part, I have no heart; so I cannot have heart disease."

"Perhaps," said the Lion thoughtfully, "if I had no heart I should not be a coward."

"Have you brains?" asked the Scarecrow.

"I suppose so. I've never looked to see," replied the Lion. "But I have been attacked by those moaning little men with ragged faces. So I guess I must have some brains."

"I am going to the Great Oz to ask him to give me some," remarked the Scarecrow, "for my head is stuffed with straw."

"And I am going to ask him to give me a heart," said the Woodman.

"And I am going to ask him to send Toto and me back to Kansas," added Dorothy.

"Do you think Oz could give me courage?" asked the Cowardly Lion.

"Just as easily as he could give me brains," said the Scarecrow.

"Or give me a heart," said the Tin Woodman.

"Or send me back to Kansas," said Dorothy.

"Then, if you don't mind, I'll go with you," said the Lion, "for my life is simply unbearable without a bit of courage."

"You will be very welcome," answered Dorothy, "for you will help to keep away the terrible creatures, living and dead, threatening this land. It seems to me you have the strength enough to fight them off."

"I do," said the Lion, "but that doesn't make me any braver, and as long as I know myself to be a coward I shall be unhappy."

So once more the little company set off upon the journey, the Lion walking with stately strides at Dorothy's side. Toto did not approve this new comrade at first, for he could not forget how nearly he had been crushed between the Lion's great jaws. But after a time he became more calm, and once again walked with his head bowed, for the sickness inside him was growing worse.

All five continued on their journey for several more hours, through dense trees and thick bush. Again from the forest around them came the bellowing moans of more undead creatures. The travelers huddled together for safety and spoke in low whispers to remain unheard.

The road began to crack and crumble in places, and once again they were forced to pick up the poor Scarecrow, who continually fell in the holes. The Tin Woodman kept his axe in front of his chest, ready for battle, just in case. It was not long before he was forced to use it.

As they rounded a corner near a little stream, the ghostly moaning grew very loud.

"They seem to be all around us," said Dorothy, "but I cannot see anything."

"Maybe they are invisible," said the Scarecrow. "For that would explain us not being able to see them."

But the Scarecrow was wrong, for a moment later the trees all around them shook, and when the group of travelers looked up into the boughs they saw a collection of dead Munchkins climbing along the branches.

"Look out!" shouted the Lion, as he spun around trying to count all the undead monsters above them. "They're everywhere!"

The tiny rotted corpses leapt out of the trees and landed on their prey's shoulders. Dorothy fell under a heap of blue and gray flesh and lost hold of her magical gun, pushing away the tiny blue heads that swooped in to bite her. The Tin Woodman swung wildly with his axe and managed to free himself rather quickly from his attackers. His axe swiftly chopped the heads off two tiny blue and gray creatures biting his tin legs. He kicked their lifeless bodies away and their blood turned the cracked Yellow Brick Road a deep orange.

The Lion had been so scared he ran up into a tree and roared from the lowest branch. But the dead Munchkins did not seem to be afraid. They stared back and moaned, "Braaaains. Feline braiiins." They didn't do it for long, however, because the Tin Woodman came over and chopped them into little bits of blood and meat. It was only when the Lion saw that Dorothy was struggling that he jumped down on all of the creatures on her back, knocking them off of her, and bit into their necks. With a wild thrashing he tore their heads from their shoulders.

Even little Toto, who was still having normal dog thoughts, managed to bite one of the monsters on the leg and trip it. It fell down and smashed its head on a rock and lay still. Toto sniffed the blood that ran from the monster's crushed head and gave it a little taste. He backed away, unsure why he liked it.

At the side of the road, the Scarecrow picked up the fallen gun, for none of the monsters were interested in him. This made him very sad, but he was happy to have the gun. He fired it straight up into the air, for he did not have the brains enough to know how to aim it. When he did, the remaining four Munchkins flew backwards in a torrent of blood. You see, this particular magic bullet broke itself into four smaller bullets, each one finding its mark. After that he picked up Dorothy and asked her if she was okay.

"I think so," said Dorothy, who checked her limbs for bites. Thankfully the Munchkins had not had a chance to sink their teeth into her before she was saved by the Lion.

"That was close," said the Tin Woodman, whose tin body was covered in Munchkin blood and new bite marks. Likewise the Scarecrow, Lion and Dorothy were coated in fresh gore. Even tiny Toto's fur had become matted with dried blood.

During the rest of that day there was no other adventure to mar the peace of their journey. Once, indeed, the Tin Woodman stepped upon a beetle that was crawling along the road, and killed the poor little thing. This made the Tin Woodman very unhappy, for he was always careful not to hurt any living creature; and as he walked along he wept several tears of sorrow and regret. These tears ran slowly down his face and over the hinges of his jaw, and there they rusted. When Dorothy presently asked him a question the Tin Woodman could not open his mouth, for his jaws were tightly rusted together. He became greatly frightened at this and made many motions to Dorothy to relieve him, but she could not understand. The Lion was also puzzled to know what was wrong. But the Scarecrow seized the oil-can from Dorothy's basket and oiled the Woodman's jaws, so that after a few moments he could talk as well as before.

"This will serve me a lesson," said he, "to look where I step. For if I should kill another bug or beetle I should surely cry again, and crying rusts my jaws so that I cannot speak."

Thereafter he walked very carefully, with his eyes on the road, and when he saw a tiny ant toiling by he would step over it, so as not to harm it. The Tin Woodman knew very well he had no heart, and therefore he took great care never to be cruel or unkind to anything that was truly living.

"You people with hearts," he said, "have something to guide you, and need never do wrong; but I have no heart, and so I must be very careful. When Oz gives me a heart of course I needn't mind so much."

7

The Journey to the Great Oz

T HEY WERE OBLIGED to camp out that night under a large tree in the forest, for there were no houses near. The tree made a good, thick covering to protect them from the living dead, and the Tin Woodman chopped a great pile of wood with his axe and Dorothy built a splendid fire that warmed her and made her feel less lonely. For a while she cleaned her magic gun. When she checked the insides, she found no bullets, and wondered where they came from. But as she knew the gun was enchanted, she did not bother to ask. As the moon rose, she and Toto ate the last of their bread, and she was happy to see he was still eating normal food. But now she did not know what they would do for breakfast.

"If you wish," said the Lion, "I will go into the forest and kill a deer for you. You can roast it by the fire, since your tastes are so peculiar that you prefer cooked food, and then you will have a very good breakfast."

"Don't! Please don't," begged the Tin Woodman. "I should certainly weep if you killed a poor deer, and then my jaws would rust again."

But the Lion went away into the forest and found his own supper, and no one ever knew what it was, for he didn't mention it. And the Scarecrow found a tree full of nuts and filled Dorothy's basket with them, so that she would not be hungry for a long time. She thought this was very kind and thoughtful of the Scarecrow, but she laughed heartily at the awkward way in which the poor creature picked up the nuts. His padded hands were so clumsy and the nuts were so small that he dropped almost as many as he put in the basket. But the Scarecrow did not mind how long it took him to fill the basket, for it enabled him to keep away from the fire, as he feared a spark might get into his straw and burn him up. So he kept a good distance away from the flames, and only came near to cover Dorothy with dry leaves when she lay down to sleep. These kept her very snug and warm, and she slept soundly until morning.

When it was daylight, the girl bathed her face in a little rippling brook, and soon after they all started toward the Emerald City.

This was to be an eventful day for the travelers. They had hardly been walking an hour when they saw before them a great ditch that crossed the road and divided the forest as far as they could see on either side. It was a very wide ditch, and when they crept up to the edge and looked into it they could see it was also very deep, and there were many big, jagged rocks at the bottom, along with some skeletons. Some of them looked human, but others were not. They had many limbs, tattered wings, and giant heads with great giant fangs protruding from their jaws.

"What are those?" asked Dorothy. "Are they giant spiders?"

"Those are Stappers," said the Lion. "The Wicked Witch conjured them many months ago by mixing all of the meanest bugs in the land. They are part spider, part scorpion, and part wasp. They roam the land hungry for blood. But these ones are long dead, so I do not fear them."

It was just then that off in the distance our travelers saw a swarm of Stappers flying in the sky. Their massive bodies had both stingers and long segmented tails with poisonous barbs on the end. There were so many of them they blocked out the clouds. In an instant they dove down into the trees, only to reemerge in the air a minute later with a family of farmers. They drove their stingers into the screaming farmers' bellies, splitting them in two, and sank their teeth into the farmers' faces. Blood rained down from the sky onto the forest. And then they were all gone, carrying the dead farmers in their legs, flying off to find more food.

"We should hurry before they come back," said the Scarecrow, "for they will surely find us if we stay still."

Dorothy looked down into the pit again. The sides were so steep that none of them could climb down, and for a moment it seemed that their journey must end.

"What shall we do?" asked Dorothy despairingly.

"I haven't the faintest idea," said the Tin Woodman, and the Lion shook his shaggy mane and looked thoughtful.

But the Scarecrow said, "We cannot fly like the Stappers, that is certain. Neither can we climb down into this great ditch. Therefore, if we cannot jump over it, we must stop where we are."

"I think I could jump over it," said the Cowardly Lion, after measuring the distance carefully in his mind.

"Then we are all right," answered the Scarecrow, "for you can carry us all over on your back, one at a time."

"Well, I'll try it," said the Lion. "Who will go first?"

"I will," declared the Scarecrow, "for, if you found that you could not jump over the gulf, Dorothy would be killed, or the Tin Woodman badly dented on the rocks below. But if I am on your back it will not matter so much, for the fall would not hurt me at all."

"I am terribly afraid of falling, myself," said the Cowardly Lion, "but I suppose there is nothing to do but try it. So get on my back and we will make the attempt."

The Scarecrow sat upon the Lion's back, and the big beast walked to the edge of the gulf and crouched down.

"Why don't you run and jump?" asked the Scarecrow.

"Because that isn't the way we Lions do these things," he replied. Then giving a great spring, he shot through the air and landed safely on the other side. They were all greatly pleased to see how easily he did it, and after the Scarecrow had got down from his back the Lion sprang across the ditch again.

Dorothy thought she would go next; so she took Toto in her arms and climbed on the Lion's back, holding tightly to his mane with one hand. The next moment it seemed as if she were flying through the air; and then, before she had time to think about it, she was safe on the other side. The Lion went back a third time and got the Tin Woodman, and then they all sat down for a few moments to give the beast a chance to rest, for his great leaps had made his breath short, and he panted like a big dog that has been running too long.

They found the forest very thick on this side, and it looked dark and gloomy. The trees here were stained a dark red with blood. Deep gouges split the tree trunks, and clumps of orange fur were stuck in the bark. Hanging from the top limb of a giant fir tree was the skinned body of a small girl. Only her hair remained, a long strand of blonde silk that blew in the breeze.

Both the Scarecrow and Tin Woodman covered their eyes at the ghastly sight.

"How horrible," said Dorothy. "Something ravaged her. Are there more lions here?"

"Not in these parts," answered the Lion. "I am sure that is the work of the Kalidahs."

"What are the Kalidahs?" asked the girl.

"They are monstrous beasts with bodies like bears and heads like tigers," replied the Lion, "and with claws so long and sharp that they could tear me in two as easily as I could kill Toto. I'm terribly afraid of the Kalidahs."

"I'm not surprised that you are," returned Dorothy. "They must be dreadful beasts to do such a thing to that poor girl."

"Unlike the undead Munchkins, the Kalidahs only want to eat your organs."

"Then I am safe," said the Tin Woodman, "for there are no more organs inside of me."

"And I am stuffed with straw," said the Scarecrow.

"Yes, but Lion and Toto and I are full of organs," said Dorothy. She wrapped her arms around herself in an attempt to feel safer.

They walked on for a while longer, spying the marks of the Kalidahs on the trees. Eventually, they sat down to rest, and Dorothy kept her magical gun at the ready in case the Kalidahs showed up.

After they had rested they started along the road of yellow brick, silently wondering, each in his own mind, if ever they would come to the end of the woods and reach the bright sunshine again. To add to their discomfort, they soon heard strange noises in the depths of the forest, and the Lion whispered to them that it was in this part of the forest that the Kalidahs lived in large wooden dens made from tree bark.

"Perhaps we should walk in a row," said the Tin Woodman, "with everyone looking in a different direction. That way we will see them coming from anywhere."

The Lion was about to reply when suddenly they came to another gulf across the road. But this one was so broad and deep that the Lion knew at once he could not leap across it. Just like the last gulf, the bottom of this one was full of skeletons from people and animals that had tried to cross it and failed.

So they sat down to consider what they should do, and after serious thought the Scarecrow said:

"Here is a great tree, standing close to the ditch. If the Tin Woodman can chop it down, so that it will fall to the other side, we can walk across it easily."

"That is a first-rate idea," said the Lion. "One would almost suspect you had brains in your head, instead of straw."

The Woodman set to work at once, and so sharp was his axe that the tree was soon chopped nearly through. Then the Lion put his strong front legs against the tree and pushed with all his might, and slowly the big tree tipped and fell with a crash across the ditch, with its top branches on the other side.

They had just started to cross this queer bridge when a sharp growl made them all look up, and to their horror they saw running toward them six great beasts with bodies like bears and heads like tigers. Their fangs were longer than Dorothy's arms and dripping with fresh blood, and from the mouth of the largest one hung the head of a small horse, its mane caught in the beast's front teeth. Their eyes glowed red like hot coals and their claws made deep gouges in the yellow bricks as they raced forward.

"They are the Kalidahs!" said the Cowardly Lion, beginning to tremble.

"Quick!" cried the Scarecrow. "Let us cross over."

So Dorothy went first, holding Toto in her arms, the Tin Woodman followed, and the Scarecrow came next. The Lion, although he was certainly afraid, turned to face the Kalidahs, and then he gave so loud and terrible a roar that Dorothy screamed and the Scarecrow fell over backward, while even the fierce beasts stopped short and looked at him in surprise.

But, seeing they were bigger than the Lion, and remembering that there were six of them and only one of him, the Kalidahs again rushed forward, and the Lion crossed over the tree and turned to see what they would do next. Without stopping an instant the fierce beasts also began to cross the tree. And the Lion said to Dorothy:

"We are lost, for they will surely tear us to pieces with their sharp claws. But stand close behind me, and I will fight them as long as I am alive."

"Wait a minute!" called the Scarecrow. He had been thinking what was best to be done, and now he asked the Woodman to chop away the end of the tree that rested on their side of the ditch. The Tin Woodman began to use his axe at once, and, just as the two closest Kalidahs were nearly across, the tree fell with a crash into the gulf, carrying the ugly, snarling brutes with it, and both were dashed to pieces on the sharp rocks at the bottom.

The remaining four, having felt the tree begin to fall, leapt with all their might and landed in a circle around the travelers.

"Quickly, shoot," said the Lion.

But as Dorothy raised her gun one of the fearsome Kalidahs knocked it from her hand with its mighty paw. This caused her to drop Toto as well, who started barking at the beasts. Before she could scoop him up the closest Kalidah snapped its jaws at the little dog, intent on chewing him up and swallowing him whole. But the Tin Woodman was quick to act, and thrust out his axe, catching it in the Kalidah's mouth and giving Toto enough time to jump out. With a mighty swing, the Tin Woodman then cut deep into the Kalidah's throat, spilling its blood all over Toto.

The beast roared with anger but fell to its belly and lay still.

The other Kalidahs were not afraid of the axe, for they were too stupid to know it was sharp, and they were too hungry for organs to care.

"Look out!" cried the Scarecrow, who was suddenly wrenched off his feet by another Kalidah. The big beast shook him back and forth and tore the stuffing out of him. But tasting no organs inside, it finally dropped the Scarecrow to the ground in a heap.

"We must run," said Dorothy, who was suddenly cut off from her friends by one of the Kalidahs. She scooped up Toto and took off into the trees. She ducked low limbs and jumped over many thorn bushes, running as fast as her little girl legs would let her. Behind her she could hear one of the big beasts crashing through the trees after her.

Back on the road, the remaining two Kalidahs attacked the Lion and the Tin Wodman. The battle was terrible, with many screams and shouts. The Tin Woodman found his entire head inside the giant maw of a Kalidah and he shrieked in fear. But the fangs could not pierce his tin head, and he was able to swing his axe into the belly of the monster, and twist it, opening up a deep cut that slowly let all of the monster's guts slip out onto its own feet.

The Lion was backed toward a tree by the largest Kalidah anyone had ever seen. It was easily the size of two Kalidahs put together. Just as it was about to slice the Lion in half with its mighty claws, the Lion remembered he was still a cat, and could climb trees very fast. He scooted up the trunk behind him, and jumped onto the Kalidah's back. He dug his own claws into the giant Kalidha's sides and bit down onto the Kalidah's neck. Fresh blood streamed from the gaping wound, and the Kalidah wailed and shook wildly. It shook so much that the Lion was thrown to the ground, right next to the gun. The giant Kalidah, its sides and neck blazing with pain, ran off into the trees, retreating from the fight.

"Where is Dorothy?" asked the Tin Woodman. He was holding the head of the Kalidah he had killed.

"She ran into the woods," shouted the Scarecrow, who was just a head on top of a pile of straw. "Someone needs to fire the gun."

The Lion, realizing he was closest to the gun, stood it upright in his paws and used his fang to squeeze the trigger. The bullet shot straight up into the air.

Dorothy was still running away from the awful beast chasing her, maneuvering as best she could through the trees. Behind her the beast's grunts and huffs grew louder and louder. Though she tried to outsmart it by squeezing under small bushes and running through tight spaces between rocks, the Kalidah merely crashed through whatever was in its way.

Without looking, she jumped off a small cliff and landed right in a giant spider web. Both she and Toto stuck fast to the sticky silk, and watched as the giant head of the Kalidah appeared slowly over the edge of the cliff above her. It licked its lips, eager for Dorothy's insides.

"Please don't eat me," she said. "I didn't do anything to you"

"The Kalidahs do not care," came an answer from behind her. She looked up and saw a giant purple Spider walking down the web toward her. It was almost as big as the Kalidah. "The Kalidahs will eat anything that has meat in it. I know because I am the same." The web shook as the Spider came closer. "We all need to eat in this dangerous forest."

Now the Kalidah leapt down off the cliff and landed in the web as well. The stupid animal was so intent on eating Dorothy it did not realize it would stick to the strands of silk. It tried in vain to crawl to her but could not move.

"How nice," said the giant Spider, "now I have two meals." The giant Spider crawled on its web and stood over the Kalidah, which tried to bite the Spider. But the Spider was able to move freely on its own web and bit down on the Kalidah's head, injecting its poisons into the beast. When the beast was still, the Spider began spinning a web around its new meal. Soon, the Kalidah was wrapped up in a silk cocoon.

"And now you," said the Spider, turning the attention of its many eyes to Dorothy. It came forth with its giant mandibles, each one dripping with the Kalidah's guts, and bent very close. "Such tender flesh," it said. Toto barked, but as he was still very sick, he couldn't muster much more than that.

"But I've never even hurt a Spider," cried Dorothy. "Don't you have enough to eat now with that big monster?"

"There is never enough."

"Then you're nothing but a glutton."

"A satisfied glutton," the Spider replied. And just then the magic bullet came speeding out of the trees and tore through the legs of the Spider, ripping each one off in succession. Black blood landed in sloppy puddles on Dorothy's face. The Spider, now nothing but a bulbous body, fell to the web and found itself stuck. "Oh no. I can't move."

"Serves you right," said Dorothy. "You are nothing but a meanie."

The bullet now came around again and severed the web wherever it held Dorothy and Toto and they fell a short way to the ground beneath them. Here, the ground was covered with the Spider's old kills: yellowing bones and corpses with sunken faces were everywhere.

"Come on, Toto, let's get back to our friends."

"But what of me," said the Spider.

"I'm sure something will come along soon and take care of you. Like you said, there is never enough."

Though it took a little while, Toto was able to sniff his way back to the Yellow Brick Road. The little doggie's tale was looking much worse, and Dorothy wondered what she would do if he tried to eat her brains. Surely she could not kill her best friend.

When they got back to the road, the Lion, Scarecrow and Tin Woodman were waiting for her, and all hugged her joyously. Dorothy thanked the Lion for shooting the Spider, and shouldered the weapon once more.

"Well," said the Cowardly Lion, drawing a long breath of relief, "I see we are going to live a little while longer, and I am glad of it, for it must be a very uncomfortable thing not to be alive. Those creatures frightened me so badly that my heart is beating yet."

"Ah," said the Tin Woodman sadly, "I wish I had a heart to beat."

This adventure made the travelers more anxious than ever to get out of the forest, and they walked so fast that Dorothy became tired, and had to ride on the Lion's back. To their great joy the trees became thinner the farther they advanced, and in the afternoon they suddenly came upon a broad river, flowing swiftly just before them. On the other side of the water they could see the road of yellow brick running through a beautiful country, with green meadows dotted with bright flowers and all the road bordered with trees hanging full of delicious fruits. They were greatly pleased to see this delightful country before them.

"How shall we cross the river?" asked Dorothy.

"That is easily done," replied the Scarecrow. "The Tin Woodman must build us a raft, so we can float to the other side."

So the Woodman took his axe and began to chop down small trees to make a raft, and while he was busy at this the Scarecrow found on the riverbank a tree full of fine fruit. This pleased Dorothy, who had eaten nothing but nuts all day, and she made a hearty meal of the ripe fruit.

But it takes time to make a raft, even when one is as industrious and untiring as the Tin Woodman, and when night came the work was not done. So they found a cozy place under the trees where they slept well until the morning; and Dorothy dreamed of the Emerald City, and of the good Wizard Oz, who would soon send her back to her own home again.

8

The Deadly Poppy Field

Our little party of travelers awakened the next morning refreshed and full of hope, and Dorothy breakfasted like a princess off peaches and plums from the trees beside the river. Behind them was the dark forest they had passed safely through, although they had suffered many discouragements; but before them was a lovely, sunny country that seemed to beckon them on to the Emerald City.

To be sure, the broad river now cut them off from this beautiful land. But the raft was nearly done, and after the Tin Woodman had cut a few more logs and fastened them together with wooden pins, they were ready to start. Dorothy sat down in the middle of the raft and held Toto in her arms. When the Cowardly Lion stepped upon the raft it tipped badly, for he was big and heavy; but the Scarecrow and the Tin Woodman stood upon the other end to steady it, and they had long poles in their hands to push the raft through the water.

They got along quite well at first, but when they reached the middle of the river the swift current swept the raft downstream, farther and farther away from the road of yellow brick. And the water grew so deep that the long poles would not touch the bottom.

"This is bad," said the Tin Woodman, "for if we cannot get to the land we shall be carried into the country of the Wicked Witch of the West, and she will enchant us and make us her slaves."

"And she may turn us into the dead and let us walk around this horrible land forever," said Dorothy.

"We must certainly get to the Emerald City if we can," the Scarecrow continued, and he pushed so hard on his long pole that it stuck fast in the mud at the bottom of the river. Then, before he could pull it out again—or let go—the raft was swept away, and the poor Scarecrow left clinging to the pole in the middle of the river.

"Good-bye!" he called after them, and they were very sorry to leave him. Indeed, the Tin Woodman began to cry, but fortunately remembered that he might rust, and so dried his tears on Dorothy's apron.

Of course this was a bad thing for the Scarecrow.

"I am now worse off than when I first met Dorothy," he thought. "Then, I was stuck on a pole in a cornfield, where I could make-believe scare the crows, at any rate. But surely there is no use for a Scarecrow stuck on a pole in the middle of a river. I am afraid I shall never have any brains, after all!"

Down the stream the raft floated, and the poor Scarecrow was left far behind. Then the Lion said:

"Something must be done to save us. I think I can swim to the shore and pull the raft after me, if you will only hold fast to the tip of my tail."

So he sprang into the water, and the Tin Woodman caught fast hold of his tail. Then the Lion began to swim with all his might toward the shore. It was hard work, although he was so big; but by and by they were drawn out of the current, and then Dorothy took the Tin Woodman's long pole and helped push the raft to the land.

They were all tired out when they reached the shore at last and stepped off upon the pretty green grass, and they also knew that the stream had carried them a long way past the road of yellow brick that led to the Emerald City.

"What shall we do now?" asked the Tin Woodman, as the Lion lay down on the grass to let the sun dry him.

"We must get back to the road, in some way," said Dorothy.

"The best plan will be to walk along the riverbank until we come to the road again," remarked the Lion.

So, when they were rested, Dorothy picked up her basket and they started along the grassy bank, to the road from which the river had carried them. It was a lovely country, with plenty of flowers and fruit trees and sunshine to cheer them, and had they not felt so sorry for the poor Scarecrow, they could have been very happy.

They walked along as fast as they could, Dorothy only stopping once to pick a beautiful flower; and after a time the Tin Woodman cried out: "Look!"

Then they all looked at the river and saw the Scarecrow perched upon his pole in the middle of the water, looking very lonely and sad.

"What can we do to save him?" asked Dorothy.

The Lion and the Woodman both shook their heads, for they did not know. So they sat down upon the bank and gazed wistfully at the Scarecrow until a Stork flew by, who, upon seeing them, stopped to rest at the water's edge.

"Who are you and where are you going?" asked the Stork.

"I am Dorothy," answered the girl, "and these are my friends, the Tin Woodman and the Cowardly Lion; and we are going to the Emerald City."

"This isn't the road," said the Stork, as she twisted her long neck and looked sharply at the queer party.

"I know it," returned Dorothy, "but we have lost the Scarecrow, and are wondering how we shall get him again."

"Where is he?" asked the Stork.

"Over there in the river," answered the little girl.

"If he wasn't so big and heavy I would get him for you," remarked the Stork.

"He isn't heavy a bit," said Dorothy eagerly, "for he is stuffed with straw; and if you will bring him back to us, we shall thank you ever and ever so much."

"Well, I'll try," said the Stork, "but if I find he is too heavy to carry I shall have to drop him in the river again."

So the big bird flew into the air and over the water till she came to where the Scarecrow was perched upon his pole. Then the Stork with her great claws grabbed the Scarecrow by the arm and carried him up into the air and back to the bank, where Dorothy and the Lion and the Tin Woodman and Toto were sitting.

When the Scarecrow found himself among his friends again, he was so happy that he hugged them all, even the Lion and Toto; and as they walked along he sang "Tol-de-ri-de-oh!" at every step, he felt so gay.

"I was afraid I should have to stay in the river forever," he said, "but the kind Stork saved me, and if I ever get any brains I shall find the Stork again and do her some kindness in return."

"That's all right," said the Stork, who was flying along beside them. "I always like to help anyone in trouble. But I must go now, for my babies are waiting in the nest for me. I hope you will find the Emerald City and that Oz will help you."

"Thank you," replied Dorothy, and then the kind Stork flew into the air and was soon out of sight.

They walked along listening to the singing of the brightly colored birds and looking at the lovely flowers which now became so thick that the ground was carpeted with them. There were big yellow and white and blue and purple blossoms, besides great clusters of scarlet poppies, which were so brilliant in color they almost dazzled Dorothy's eyes.

"Aren't they beautiful?" the girl asked, as she breathed in the spicy scent of the bright flowers.

"I suppose so," answered the Scarecrow. "When I have brains, I shall probably like them better."

"If I only had a heart, I should love them," added the Tin Woodman.

"I always did like flowers," said the Lion. "They of seem so helpless and frail. But there are none in the forest so bright as these."

They now came upon more and more of the big scarlet poppies, and fewer and fewer of the other flowers; and soon they found themselves in the midst of a great meadow of poppies. Now it is well known that when there are many of these flowers together their odor is so powerful that anyone who breathes it falls asleep, and if the sleeper is not carried away from the scent of the flowers, he sleeps on and on forever. But Dorothy did not know this, nor could she get away from the bright red flowers that were everywhere about; so presently her eyes grew heavy and she felt she must sit down to rest and to sleep.

But the Tin Woodman would not let her do this.

"We must hurry and get back to the road of yellow brick before dark," he said; and the Scarecrow agreed with him. So they kept walking until Dorothy could stand no longer. Her eyes closed in spite of herself and she forgot where she was and fell among the poppies, fast asleep.

"What shall we do?" asked the Tin Woodman.

"If we leave her here she will die," said the Lion. "The smell of the flowers is killing us all. I myself can scarcely keep my eyes open, and the dog is asleep already."

It was true; Toto had fallen down beside his little mistress. But the Scarecrow and the Tin Woodman, not being made of flesh, were not troubled by the scent of the flowers.

"Run fast," said the Scarecrow to the Lion, "and get out of this deadly flower bed as soon as you can. We will bring the little girl with us, but if you should fall asleep you are too big to be carried."

So the Lion aroused himself and bounded forward as fast as he could go. In a moment he was out of sight.

"Let us make a chair with our hands and carry her," said the Scarecrow. So they picked up Toto and put the dog in Dorothy's lap, and then they made a chair with their hands for the seat and their arms for the arms and carried the sleeping girl between them through the flowers.

On and on they walked, and it seemed that the great carpet of deadly flowers that surrounded them would never end. They followed the bend of the river, and at last came upon their friend the Lion, lying fast asleep among the poppies. The flowers had been too strong for the huge beast and he had given up at last, and fallen only a short distance from the end of the poppy bed, where the sweet grass spread in beautiful green fields before them.

"We can do nothing for him," said the Tin Woodman, sadly; "for he is much too heavy to lift. We must leave him here to sleep on forever, and perhaps he will dream that he has found courage at last."

"I'm sorry," said the Scarecrow. "The Lion was a very good comrade for one so cowardly. But let us go on."

They carried the sleeping girl to a pretty spot beside the river, far enough from the poppy field to prevent her breathing any more of the poison of the flowers, and here they laid her gently on the soft grass and waited for the fresh breeze to waken her.

9

The Queen of the Field Mice

"WE CANNOT BE far from the road of yellow brick, now," remarked the Scarecrow, as he stood beside the girl, "for we have come nearly as far as the river carried us away."

The Tin Woodman was about to reply when he heard a low growl, and turning his head (which worked beautifully on hinges) he saw a strange beast come bounding over the grass toward them. It was, indeed, a great yellow Wildcat, and the Woodman thought it must be chasing something, for its ears were lying close to its head and its mouth was wide open, showing two rows of ugly teeth, while its red eyes glowed like balls of fire. As it came nearer the Tin Woodman saw that running before the beast was a little gray field mouse, and although he had no heart he knew it was wrong for the Wildcat to try to kill such a pretty, harmless creature.

So the Woodman raised his axe, and as the Wildcat ran by he gave it a quick blow that cut the beast's head clean off from its body, and it rolled over at his feet in two pieces.

The field mouse, now that it was freed from its enemy, stopped short; and coming slowly up to the Woodman it said, in a squeaky little voice:

"Oh, thank you! Thank you ever so much for saving my life."

"Don't speak of it, I beg of you," replied the Woodman. "I have no heart, you know, so I am careful to help all those who may need a friend, even if it happens to be only a mouse."

"Only a mouse!" cried the little animal, indignantly. "Why, I am a Queen—the Queen of all the Field Mice!"

"Oh, indeed," said the Woodman, making a bow.

"Therefore you have done a great deed, as well as a brave one, in saving my life," added the Queen.

At that moment several mice were seen running up as fast as their little legs could carry them, and when they saw their Queen they exclaimed:

"Oh, your Majesty, we thought you would be killed and come back to eat us! How did you manage to escape the great Wildcat?" They all bowed so low to the little Queen that they almost stood upon their heads.

"This funny tin man," she answered, "killed the Wildcat and saved my life. So hereafter you must all serve him, and obey his slightest wish."

"We will!" cried all the mice, in a shrill chorus. And then they scampered in all directions, for Toto had awakened from his sleep, and seeing all these mice around him he gave one bark of delight and jumped right into the middle of the group. Toto was having fits of hunger for flesh now, and knew even in his sickening state he could get the brains of the field mice.

But the Tin Woodman caught the dog in his arms and held him tight, while he called to the mice, "Come back! Come back! Toto shall not hurt you."

At this the Queen of the Mice stuck her head out from underneath a clump of grass and asked, in a timid voice, "Are you sure he will not bite us?"

"I will not let him," said the Woodman; "so do not be afraid."

One by one the mice came creeping back, and Toto did not bark again, although he tried to get out of the Woodman's arms, and would have bitten him had he not known very well he was made of tin. Finally one of the biggest mice spoke.

"Is there anything we can do," it asked, "to repay you for saving the life of our Queen?"

"Nothing that I know of," answered the Woodman; but the Scarecrow, who had been trying to think, but could not because his head was stuffed with straw, said, quickly, "Oh, yes; you can save our friend, the Cowardly Lion, who is asleep in the poppy bed."

"A Lion!" cried the little Queen. "Why, he would eat us all up."

"Oh, no," declared the Scarecrow, "this Lion is a coward."

"Really?" asked the Mouse.

"He says so himself," answered the Scarecrow, "and he would never hurt anyone who is our friend. If you will help us to save him I promise that he shall treat you all with kindness."

"Very well," said the Queen, "we trust you. But what shall we do?"

"Are there many of these mice which call you Queen and are willing to obey you?"

"Oh, yes; there are thousands," she replied.

"Then send for them all to come here as soon as possible, and let each one bring a long piece of string."

The Queen turned to the mice that attended her and told them to go at once and get all her people. As soon as they heard her orders they ran away in every direction as fast as possible.

"Now," said the Scarecrow to the Tin Woodman, "you must go to those trees by the riverside and make a truck that will carry the Lion."

So the Woodman went at once to the trees and began to work; and he soon made a truck out of the limbs of trees, from which he chopped away all the leaves and branches. He fastened it together with wooden pegs and made the four wheels out of short pieces of a big tree trunk. So fast and so well did he work that by the time the mice began to arrive the truck was all ready for them.

They came from all directions, and there were thousands of them: big mice and little mice and middle-sized mice; and each one brought a piece of string in his mouth. It was about this time that Dorothy woke from her long sleep and opened her eyes. She was greatly astonished to find herself lying upon the grass, with thousands of mice standing around and looking at her timidly.

But the Scarecrow told her about everything, and turning to the dignified little Mouse, he said:

"Permit me to introduce to you her Majesty, the Queen."

Dorothy nodded gravely and the Queen made a curtsy, after which she became quite friendly with the little girl. Dorothy explained how they were going to see the Great Oz to get a brain, a heart, courage, and figure out a way to save the land from the Witch's plague. "And most of all," Dorothy concluded, "to get me back to Kansas."

The Scarecrow and the Woodman now began to fasten the mice to the truck, using the strings they had brought. One end of a string was tied around the neck of each mouse and the other end to the truck. Of course the truck was a thousand times bigger than any of the mice who were to draw it; but when all the mice had been harnessed, they were able to pull it quite easily. Even the Scarecrow and the Tin Woodman could sit on it, and were drawn swiftly by their queer little horses to the place where the Lion lay asleep.

After a great deal of hard work, for the Lion was heavy, they managed to get him up on the truck. Then the Queen hurriedly gave her people the order to start, for she feared if the mice stayed among the poppies too long they also would fall asleep.

At first the little creatures, many though they were, could hardly stir the heavily loaded truck; but the Woodman and the Scarecrow both pushed from behind, and they got along better.

They were almost to the edge of the poppy field when they saw the first group of undead Munchkins shambling through the flowers.

"It appears we have company," said the Tin Woodman. "And there are a lot of them."

From the edge of the poppy field Dorothy yelled for her friends to hurry up, but half way through her cries she felt something scampering up her legs. She looked down and saw hordes of bloody, decaying mice covering them. She screamed and kicked wildly, throwing the undead mice into the air. But more came out of the grass, their tiny teeth yellow and slick.

"Oh no," said the Queen of the Field Mice. "It is our dead, come back to eat us. Every time we think we've outrun them they return."

The Tin Woodman and Scarecrow heaved with all their might to get the Lion out of the poppies, but it was only an instant later that the first undead Munchkin leapt at the Scarecrow and knocked him over. "Help me! Help Me!"

The Tin Woodman swung is axe and took the little monster's head clean off. But now two more had arrived and pushed toward the sleeping Lion. "They want the Lion's brains."

From the edge of the field, Dorothy screamed again, and grabbed three mice in her hand and bashed them on a rock. Their little undead bones flipped into the air and landed in her long, braided hair. Toto scooped up two in his mouth and bit them in half, cracking their tiny skulls in his teeth.

The Queen of the Field Mice let go of the truck and raced to help Dorothy, rolling into a ball and knocking back several of her undead kin. Dorothy helped by stepping as hard as she could on the swarming mice. Their bodies crunched under her feet and she used her magic rifle as a club and hit them away.

Three undead Munchkins had gotten on top of the Lion and were about to tear into his flesh when the Tin Woodman wedged his axe into their heads. He grabbed one more little blue man with glazed eyes and squeezed its head with all his might. The Tin Woodman, being made of a substance stronger than flesh, had a good deal of strength, and when he squeezed the little monster's head it caved in. Brains dribbled out of the Munchkin's ears.

There were more dead Munchkins coming, but they were still a little ways off. "Quickly, we need the Lion to help us," said the Tin

Woodman, and urged the mice and the Scarecrow to pull with all their strength. It was strenuous work but they put all their might into it and a few seconds later they were out of the poppy field.

Dorothy was holding many dead mice in her hand, and at her feet the Queen of the Field Mice bared her teeth and swiped at any undead mouse that got close.

"There are too many of them," Dorothy screamed. Beside her, Toto bit the head off one of the small rodents that had scurried onto his back.

Dorothy finally fired her gun, but it did not shoot, for it had gotten very wet in the river and had not dried yet. "Curses!" she screamed.

Now the Lion awoke, and yawned, and took in the scene around him. "What is going on?" he asked. Before anyone could answer one of the decaying little Munchkins stumbled out of the poppy field and bit at the giant cat's face. The Lion, used to flinching at the slightest danger, dodged the attack as the Scarecrow picked up a rock near his feet and bashed the creature over the head. Again and again he smashed the rock against the thing's skull, until its pink brains oozed through a giant crack over its eyes. It fell down dead, and the Scarecrow could only stare in wonder at the lovely brains he wished he could have. Tentatively, he reached out and touched the pink mess, wondering at their magical powers of thought.

"Quickly, everyone on my back," the Lion said. "I can run faster than these creatures and get us to safety."

"But I cannot leave my mice," replied the Queen. "I must stay and fight. You go on, and tell the Great Wizard to rid us of this plague. Take this whistle. If you need us again, just call."

"Please be safe," said Dorothy, putting the whistle in her pocket and climbing onto the Lion's back.

"I will," replied the Queen, and with a tiny roar she ran back into the battle where her family bit and scratched at the undead mice that scurried over the ground. Their tiny dying squeaks and peeps of pain lifted into the air like the rusty hinges of a thousand old doors. The last thing Dorothy saw was the Queen rolling around with six or seven bloodthirsty foes. The outcome did not look favorable.

With all of his comrades on his back, the Lion was terribly weighted down, but he did not want to get bitten by the dead Munchkins, and so he ran as fast as he could, putting a great distance between himself and the attackers. Dorothy held Toto in her arms and cried as they ran, for the little dog's eyes were turning a dismal yellow and glazing over. They needed to get to the Great Oz immediately.

1o

The Guardian of the Gates

IT WAS SOME time before the Cowardly Lion awakened, for he had lain among the poppies a long while, breathing in their deadly fragrance; but when he did open his eyes and roll off the truck he was very glad to find himself still alive.

"I ran as fast as I could," he said, sitting down and yawning, "but the flowers were too strong for me. How did you get me out?"

Then they told him of the field mice, and how they had generously saved him from death; and the Cowardly Lion laughed, and said:

"I have always thought myself very big and terrible; yet such little things as flowers came near to killing me, and such small animals as mice have saved my life. How strange it all is! But, comrades, what shall we do now?"

"We must journey on until we find the road of yellow brick again," said Dorothy, "and then we can keep on to the Emerald City."

So, the Lion being fully refreshed, and feeling quite himself again, they all started upon the journey, greatly enjoying the walk through the soft, fresh grass; and it was not long before they reached the road of yellow brick and turned again toward the Emerald City where the Great Oz dwelt.

The road was smooth and well paved, now, and the country about was beautiful, so that the travelers rejoiced in leaving the forest far behind, and with it the many dangers they had met in its gloomy shades. Once more they could see fences built beside the road; but these were painted green, and when they came to a small house, in which a farmer evidently lived, that also was painted green. They passed by several of these houses during the afternoon, and sometimes people came to the doors and looked at them as if they would like to ask questions; but no one came near them nor spoke to them because of the great Lion, of which they were very much afraid. The people were all dressed in clothing of a lovely emerald-green color and wore peaked hats like those of the Munchkins.

"This must be the Land of Oz," said Dorothy, "and we are surely getting near the Emerald City."

"Yes," answered the Scarecrow. "Everything is green here, while in the country of the Munchkins blue was the favorite color. But the people do not seem to be as friendly as the Munchkins, and I'm afraid we shall be unable to find a place to pass the night."

"I should like something to eat besides fruit," said the girl, "and I'm sure Toto is near to death. Let us stop at the next house and talk to the people."

So, when they came to a good-sized farmhouse, Dorothy walked boldly up to the door and knocked.

A woman opened it just far enough to look out, and said, "What do you want, child, and why is that great Lion with you?"

"We wish to pass the night with you, if you will allow us," answered Dorothy; "and the Lion is my friend and comrade, and would not hurt you for the world."

"Is he tame?" asked the woman, opening the door a little wider.

"Oh, yes," said the girl, "and he is a great coward, too. He will be more afraid of you than you are of him."

"Well," said the woman, after thinking it over and taking another peep at the Lion, "if that is the case you may come in, and I will give you some supper and a place to sleep."

So they all entered the house, where there were, besides the woman, two children and a man. The man had hurt his leg, and was lying on the couch in a corner. They seemed greatly surprised to see so strange a company, and while the woman was busy laying the table the man asked:

"Where are you all going?"

"To the Emerald City," said Dorothy, "to see the Great Oz."

"Oh, indeed!" exclaimed the man. "Are you sure that Oz will see you?"

"Why not?" she replied.

"Why, it is said that he never lets anyone come into his presence. I have been to the Emerald City many times, and it is a beautiful and wonderful place; but I have never been permitted to see the Great Oz, nor do I know of any living person who has seen him."

"Does he never go out?" asked the Scarecrow.

"Never. He sits day after day in the great Throne Room of his Palace, and even those who wait upon him do not see him face to face."

"What is he like?" asked the girl.

"That is hard to tell," said the man thoughtfully. "You see, Oz is a Great Wizard, and can take on any form he wishes. So that some say he looks like a bird; and some say he looks like an elephant; and some say he looks like a cat. To others he appears as a beautiful fairy, or a brownie, or in any other form that pleases him. But who the real Oz is, when he is in his own form, no living person can tell."

"That is very strange," said Dorothy, "but we must try, in some way, to see him, or we shall have made our journey for nothing."

"Why do you wish to see the terrible Oz?" asked the man.

"I want him to give me some brains," said the Scarecrow eagerly.

"Oh, Oz could do that easily enough," declared the man." He has more brains than he needs."

"And I want him to give me a heart," said the Tin Woodman.

"That will not trouble him," continued the man, "for Oz has a large collection of hearts, of all sizes and shapes."

"And I want him to give me courage," said the Cowardly Lion.

"Oz keeps a great pot of courage in his Throne Room," said the man, "which he has covered with a golden plate, to keep it from running over. He will be glad to give you some."

"And I want him to send me back to Kansas," said Dorothy.

"Where is Kansas?" asked the man, with surprise.

"I don't know," replied Dorothy sorrowfully, "but it is my home, and I'm sure it's somewhere."

"Very likely. Well, Oz can do anything; so I suppose he will find Kansas for you. But first you must get to see him, and that will be a hard task; for the Great Wizard does not like to see anyone, and he usually has his own way. But what do YOU want?" he continued, speaking to Toto.

And once again this reminded Dorothy of her promise to the Good Witch. "Toto has been bitten by one of those dreadful brain-eating Munchkins. We must ask Oz to save him and this land."

"Well now that might be a problem," said the man, "for Oz can pretty much do anything but I do not know if he can bring anything back from the dead. What we must do for this dog is get the deadly virus out of his system."

"How do we do that?"

"I will draw some of my own blood and inject it into him."

"Mixing human blood and dog blood?"

"Yes, for you see I am laid up on this couch after getting bitten by one of those deadly Munchkins. I have been sick for days but I am recovering. It seems I have an immunity to their virus."

"What if it doesn't work?"

"Then I can do nothing more for you. But it is worth a shot."

"If you have an imm . . ." Dorothy struggled with the large word.

"Immunity."

"Yes, if you have that, then you can help save the land."

"I have thought of that, yes, but I am not strong enough yet to visit the neighboring villages and tell them. I am hoping that in a few days I will be as fit as a fiddle and will make a trek to see if I can help."

"Wonderful!" yelled Dorothy, for she was happy that she might have found a cure for Toto and the land.

The woman now called to them that supper was ready, so they gathered around the table and Dorothy ate some delicious porridge and a dish of scrambled eggs and a plate of nice white bread, and enjoyed her meal. The Lion ate some of the porridge, but did not care for it, saying it was made from oats and oats were food for horses, not for lions. The Scarecrow and the Tin Woodman ate nothing at all. Toto ate a little of everything, and then went out to the barn with the man alone, for the man forbade Dorothy to watch the procedure.

The woman now gave Dorothy a bed to sleep in, and the little girl worried about Toto all night. The Lion guarded the door of her room so she might not be disturbed. The Scarecrow and the Tin Woodman stood up in a corner and kept quiet all night, although of course they could not sleep.

The next morning, as soon as the sun was up, Dorothy asked after Toto and the man informed her that the dog was sleeping. He said it might be a couple of days before the dog would be up and about. Dorothy asked if she could see Toto and the man took her to him. In the barn, Toto was in a cage, sleeping on a giant pillow. There was a bald spot on his head and a tiny scar. As the little dog slept, his legs twitched, dreaming of chasing something. Dorothy hoped it wasn't anything human.

"Can I hold him?"

"I would wait," said the man. "It is too early to tell if he is dangerous. As I began the procedure he tried very hard to bite me, and his eyes had just about turned completely opaque. Even if my own antidote works, we may not have been quick enough."

For the rest of the day Dorothy sat by the cage and cleaned her gun. She talked to Toto and told him of all the festive activities they would do together once they got back to Kansas.

The small dog did not wake up, and his breathing was slow, but at least he was still alive.

The group of travelers spent three more nights with the man, his wife and their children. At night they talked about many things, and Dorothy told them all about Kansas. To them, it seemed a more magical place than Oz.

"And you say there are no monsters?"

"None that I have seen," replied Dorothy. "Although Old Mr. Johnson, the town mailman, can be quite crabby."

On the third night, the man said he was feeling much better and would begin traveling to the nearby villages to inform them of his antibodies. But at some point in the night, when everyone was sleeping, the man heard noises outside and went to investigate. Suddenly, he found himself surrounded by five of the undead Munchkins, each one gray and bloated.

Knowing he could not catch the virus, he didn't bother to rush back to the house and get his gun, but instead began beating the monsters with his own fists. Soon his knuckles were bloody and swollen, but he could not hit them hard enough to destroy their brains. When he stumbled, the little monsters swarmed him and bit into his flesh, tearing off his nose, ears and lips. He screamed and tried to run away but they held him fast and tore off long strips of meat from his neck and back. Finally, Dorothy came running outside with her gun, which was now quite dry, and shot at them. The bullet caught fire in midair and drenched all of the Munchkins in an arc of blue flame. They fell to the ground, popping and sizzling as the fire reduced them to ash.

For the next week the man's wife cried, and Dorothy, the Scarecrow, the Lion and the Tin Woodman kept watch over her. They buried the man out in the field behind the house. To be safe, they watched the grave the first few nights but the man did not rise from the dead. He had simply died from trauma and blood loss.

This made Dorothy sad, for she did not know if she would meet anyone else with a cure for the plague.

A few days later Dorothy heard barking in the barn and went to check on Toto. The little dog's eyes were back to normal and he was spry and grinning. Dorothy took him from the cage and hugged him close. "Oh, Toto, I am so glad you are better." She was so happy to have her best friend back to normal that she played with the little dog outside and then gave him plenty to eat. He no longer had any urge to eat brains, although he did still like to chase smaller creatures, just to show them who was boss. If only the man had not died then his cure might have helped save Oz like it had saved Toto. As it was, they were back to having to ask the wizard for help.

Dorothy thanked the woman for her hospitality and told her she would never forget her husband's bravery, and soon after the travelers started on their way again. As they walked they saw a beautiful green glow in the sky just before them.

"That must be the Emerald City," said Dorothy.

As they walked on, the green glow became brighter and brighter, and it seemed that at last they were nearing the end of their travels. Yet it was afternoon before they came to the great wall that surrounded the City. It was high and thick and of a bright green color.

In front of them, and at the end of the road of yellow brick, was a big gate, all studded with emeralds that glittered so in the sun that even the painted eyes of the Scarecrow were dazzled by their brilliancy.

There was a bell beside the gate, and Dorothy pushed the button and heard a silvery tinkle sound within. Then the big gate swung slowly open, and they all passed through and found themselves in a high arched room, the walls of which glistened with countless emeralds.

Before them stood a little man about the same size as the Munchkins. He was clothed all in green, from his head to his feet, and even his skin was of a greenish tint. At his side was a large green box.

When he saw Dorothy and her companions the man asked, "What do you wish in the Emerald City?"

"We came here to see the Great Oz," said Dorothy.

The man was so surprised at this answer that he sat down to think it over.

"It has been many years since anyone asked me to see Oz," he said, shaking his head in perplexity. "He is powerful and terrible, and if you come on an idle or foolish errand to bother the wise reflections of the Great Wizard, he might be angry and destroy you all in an instant."

"But it is not a foolish errand, nor an idle one," replied the Scarecrow; "it is important. And we have been told that Oz is a good Wizard."

"So he is," said the green man, "and he rules the Emerald City wisely and well. But to those who are not honest, or who approach him from curiosity, he is most terrible, and few have ever dared ask to see his face. I am the Guardian of the Gates, and since you demand to see the Great Oz I must take you to his Palace. But first you must put on the spectacles."

"Why?" asked Dorothy.

"Because if you did not wear spectacles the brightness and glory of the Emerald City would blind you. Even those who live in the City must wear spectacles night and day. They are all locked on, for Oz so ordered it when the City was first built, and I have the only key that will unlock them."

He opened the big box, and Dorothy saw that it was filled with spectacles of every size and shape. All of them had green glasses in them. The Guardian of the Gates found a pair that would just fit Dorothy and put them over her eyes. There were two golden bands fastened to them that passed around the back of her head, where they were locked together by a little key that was at the end of a chain the Guardian of the Gates wore around his neck. When they were on, Dorothy could not take them off had she wished, but of course she did not wish to be blinded by the glare of the Emerald City, so she said nothing.

Then the green man fitted spectacles for the Scarecrow and the Tin Woodman and the Lion, and even on little Toto; and all were locked fast with the key.

Then the Guardian of the Gates put on his own glasses and told them he was ready to show them to the Palace. Taking a big golden key from a peg on the wall, he opened another gate, and they all followed him through the portal into the streets of the Emerald City.

11

The Emerald City of Oz

Even with eyes protected by the green spectacles, Dorothy and her friends were at first dazzled by the brilliancy of the wonderful City. The streets were lined with beautiful houses all built of green marble and studded everywhere with sparkling emeralds. They walked over a pavement of the same green marble, and where the blocks were joined together were rows of emeralds, set closely, and glittering in the brightness of the sun. The window panes were of green glass; even the sky above the City had a green tint, and the rays of the sun were green.

There were many people—men, women, and children—walking about, and these were all dressed in green clothes and had greenish skins. They looked at Dorothy and her strangely assorted company with wondering eyes, and the children all ran away and hid behind their mothers when they saw the Lion; but no one spoke to them. Many shops stood in the street, and Dorothy saw that everything in them was green. Green candy and green pop corn were offered for sale, as well as green shoes, green hats, and green clothes of all sorts. At one place a man was selling green lemonade, and when the children bought it Dorothy could see that they paid for it with green pennies.

There seemed to be no horses nor animals of any kind; the men carried things around in little green carts, which they pushed before them. Everyone seemed happy and contented and prosperous.

The Guardian of the Gates led them through the streets until they came to a big building, exactly in the middle of the City, which was the Palace of Oz, the Great Wizard. There was a soldier before the door, dressed in a green uniform and wearing a long green beard.

"Here are strangers," said the Guardian of the Gates to him," and they demand to see the Great Oz."

"Step inside," answered the soldier, "and I will carry your message to him."

So they passed through the Palace Gates and were led into a big room with a green carpet and lovely green furniture set with emeralds. The soldier made them all wipe their feet upon a green mat before entering this room, and when they were seated he said politely:

"Please make yourselves comfortable while I go to the door of the Throne Room and tell Oz you are here."

They had to wait a long time before the soldier returned. When, at last, he came back, Dorothy asked:

"Have you seen Oz?"

"Oh, no," returned the soldier; "I have never seen him. But I spoke to him as he sat behind his screen and gave him your message. He said he will grant you an audience, if you so desire; but each one of you must enter his presence alone, and he will admit but one each day. Therefore, as you must remain in the Palace for several days, I will have you shown to rooms where you may rest in comfort after your journey."

"Thank you," replied the girl; "that is very kind of Oz."

The soldier now blew upon a green whistle, and at once a young girl, dressed in a pretty green silk gown, entered the room. She had lovely green hair and green eyes, and she bowed low before Dorothy as she said, "Follow me and I will show you your room."

So Dorothy said good-bye to all her friends except Toto, and taking the dog in her arms followed the green girl through seven passages and up three flights of stairs until they came to a room at the front of the Palace. It was the sweetest little room in the world, with a soft comfortable bed that had sheets of green silk and a green velvet counterpane. There was a tiny fountain in the middle of the room that shot a spray of green perfume into the air, to fall back into a beautifully carved green marble basin. Beautiful green flowers stood in the windows, and there was a shelf with a row of little green books. When Dorothy had time to open these books she found them full of queer green pictures that made her laugh, they were so funny.

In a wardrobe were many green dresses, made of silk and satin and velvet; and all of them fitted Dorothy exactly.

"Make yourself perfectly at home," said the green girl, "and if you wish for anything ring the bell. Oz will send for you tomorrow morning."

She left Dorothy alone and went back to the others. These she also led to rooms, and each one of them found himself lodged in a very pleasant part of the Palace. Of course this politeness was wasted on the Scarecrow; for when he found himself alone in his room he stood stupidly in one spot, just within the doorway, to wait till morning. It would not rest him to lie down, and he could not close his eyes; so he remained all night staring at a little spider which was weaving its web in a corner of the room, just as if it were not one of the most wonderful rooms in the world.

The Tin Woodman lay down on his bed from force of habit, for he remembered when he was made of flesh; but not being able to sleep, he passed the night moving his joints up and down to make sure they kept in good working order. The Lion would have preferred a bed of dried leaves in the forest, and did not like being shut up in a room; but he had too much sense to let this worry him, so he sprang upon the bed and rolled himself up like a cat and purred himself asleep in a minute.

The next morning, after breakfast, the green maiden came to fetch Dorothy, and she dressed her in one of the prettiest gowns, made of green brocaded satin. Dorothy put on a green silk apron and tied a green ribbon around Toto's neck, and they started for the Throne Room of the Great Oz.

First they came to a great hall in which were many ladies and gentlemen of the court, all dressed in rich costumes. These people had nothing to do but talk to each other, but they always came to wait outside the Throne Room every morning, although they were never permitted to see Oz. As Dorothy entered they looked at her curiously, and one of them whispered:

"Are you really going to look upon the face of Oz the Terrible?"

"Of course," answered the girl, "if he will see me."

"Oh, he will see you," said the soldier who had taken her message to the Wizard, "although he does not like to have people ask to see him. Indeed, at first he was angry and said I should send you back where you came from. Then he asked me what you looked like, and when I mentioned your silver shoes he was very much interested. At last I told him about the mark upon your forehead, and he decided he would admit you to his presence."

Just then a bell rang, and the green girl said to Dorothy, "That is the signal. You must go into the Throne Room alone."

She opened a little door and Dorothy walked boldly through and found herself in a wonderful place. It was a big, round room with a high arched roof, and the walls and ceiling and floor were covered with large emeralds set closely together. In the center of the roof was a great light, as bright as the sun, which made the emeralds sparkle in a wonderful manner.

But what interested Dorothy most was the big throne of green marble that stood in the middle of the room. It was shaped like a chair and sparkled with gems, as did everything else. In the center of the chair was an enormous Head, without a body to support it or any arms or legs whatever. There was no hair upon this head, but it had eyes and a nose and mouth, and was much bigger than the head of the biggest giant.

As Dorothy gazed upon this in wonder and fear, the eyes turned slowly and looked at her sharply and steadily. Then the mouth moved, and Dorothy heard a voice say:

"I am Oz, the Great and Terrible. Who are you, and why do you seek me?"

It was not such an awful voice as she had expected to come from the big Head; so she took courage and answered:

"I am Dorothy, the Small and Meek. I have come to you for help."

The eyes looked at her thoughtfully for a full minute. Then said the voice:

"Where did you get the silver shoes? Is that blood on them?"

"It is, and I got them from the Wicked Witch of the East, when my house fell on her and killed her," she replied.

"Where did you get the mark upon your forehead?" continued the voice.

"That is where the Good Witch of the North kissed me when she bade me good-bye and sent me to you," said the girl.

Again the eyes looked at her sharply, and they saw she was telling the truth. Then Oz asked, "What do you wish me to do?"

"Send me back to Kansas, where my Aunt Em and Uncle Henry are," she answered earnestly. "I don't like your country, it is overrun with dead things. And I am sure Aunt Em will be dreadfully worried over my being away so long."

"Dead things?"

"Oh yes. Undead nasty little Munchkins that eat your brains. The Wicked Witch of the West cursed the land so that anything that dies comes back hungry for living flesh. And if they bite you, you turn into the walking dead as well. It's quite disgusting and we've had several close calls with them just getting here. Do you not know of this problem?"

The eyes winked three times, and then they turned up to the ceiling and down to the floor and rolled around so queerly that they seemed to see every part of the room. And at last they looked at Dorothy again. "I have heard rumors, but I have yet to see these dead things."

"But they are everywhere. Will you please put a stop to it and send me back to Kansas?"

"Why should I do this for you?" asked Oz.

"Because you are strong and I am weak; because you are a Great Wizard and I am only a little girl."

"But you were strong enough to kill the Wicked Witch of the East," said Oz.

"That just happened," returned Dorothy simply; "I could not help it."

"And what of the undead? Have you killed them?"

"Well, yes, I suppose, but they are not alive, and they want to eat us."

"Well," said the Head, "you are now just splitting hairs, little girl. So I will give you my answer. You have no right to expect me to do these things for you unless you do something for me in return. In this country everyone must pay for everything he gets. If you wish me to use my magic powers to fulfill your requests then you must do something for me first. Help me and I will help you."

"What must I do?" asked the girl.

"Kill the Wicked Witch of the West," answered Oz.

"But I cannot!" exclaimed Dorothy, greatly surprised.

"You killed the Witch of the East and you wear the silver shoes, which bear a powerful charm. There is now but one Wicked Witch left in all this land, and it is she that controls the curse. If I fix it now, she will only start it again, and then I will have wasted my time. Do this so that I may return the undead to their graves and I will send you home. But not before."

The little girl began to weep, she was so much disappointed; and the eyes winked again and looked upon her anxiously, as if the Great Oz felt that she could help him if she would.

"I never killed anything, willingly," she sobbed. "Even if I wanted to, how could I kill the Wicked Witch? If you, who are Great and Terrible, cannot kill her yourself, how do you expect me to do it?"

"I do not know," said the Head; "but that is my answer, and until the Wicked Witch dies this land will remain plagued, and you will remain in it. Remember that the Witch is Wicked—tremendously Wicked—and ought to be killed. Now go, and do not ask to see me again until you have done your task."

Sorrowfully Dorothy left the Throne Room and went back where the Lion and the Scarecrow and the Tin Woodman were waiting to hear what Oz had said to her. "There is no hope for me," she said sadly, "for Oz will not grant my wishes until I have killed the Wicked Witch of the West; and that I can never do."

Her friends were sorry, but could do nothing to help her; so Dorothy went to her own room and lay down on the bed and cried herself to sleep.

The next morning the soldier with the green whiskers came to the Scarecrow and said:

"Come with me, for Oz has sent for you."

So the Scarecrow followed him and was admitted into the great Throne Room, where he saw, sitting in the emerald throne, a most lovely Lady. She was dressed in green silk gauze and wore upon her flowing green locks a crown of jewels. Growing from her shoulders were wings, gorgeous in color and so light that they fluttered if the slightest breath of air reached them.

When the Scarecrow had bowed, as prettily as his straw stuffing would let him, before this beautiful creature, she looked upon him sweetly, and said:

"I am Oz, the Great and Terrible. Who are you, and why do you seek me?"

Now the Scarecrow, who had expected to see the great Head Dorothy had told him of, was much astonished; but he answered her bravely.

"I am only a Scarecrow, stuffed with straw. Therefore I have no brains, and I come to you praying that you will put brains in my head instead of straw, so that I may become as much a man as any other in your dominions."

"Why do you want brains? They will only be eaten at some point."

"I know this, but that means I will have been a real man. And that is all I wish."

"Why should I do this for you?" asked the Lady.

"Because you are wise and powerful, and no one else can help me," answered the Scarecrow.

"I never grant favors without some return," said Oz; "but this much I will promise. If you will kill for me the Wicked Witch of the West, I will bestow upon you a great many brains, and such good brains that you will be the wisest man in all the Land of Oz."

"I thought you asked Dorothy to kill the Witch," said the Scarecrow, in surprise.

"So I did. I don't care who kills her. But until she is dead I will not grant your wish. Now go, and do not seek me again until you have earned the brains you so greatly desire."

The Scarecrow went sorrowfully back to his friends and told them what Oz had said; and Dorothy was surprised to find that the Great

Wizard was not a Head, as she had seen him, but a lovely Lady.

"All the same," said the Scarecrow, "she needs a heart as much as the Tin Woodman."

On the next morning the soldier with the green whiskers came to the Tin Woodman and said:

"Oz has sent for you. Follow me."

So the Tin Woodman followed him and came to the great Throne Room. He did not know whether he would find Oz a lovely Lady or a Head, but he hoped it would be the lovely Lady. "For," he said to himself, "if it is the head, I am sure I shall not be given a heart, since a head has no heart of its own and therefore cannot feel for me. But if it is the lovely Lady I shall beg hard for a heart, for all ladies are themselves said to be kindly hearted.

But when the Woodman entered the great Throne Room he saw neither the Head nor the Lady, for Oz had taken the shape of a most terrible Beast. It was nearly as big as an elephant, and the green throne seemed hardly strong enough to hold its weight. The Beast had a head like that of a rhinoceros, only there were five eyes in its face. There were five long arms growing out of its body, and it also had five long, slim legs. Thick, woolly hair covered every part of it, and a more dreadful-looking monster could not be imagined. It was fortunate the Tin Woodman had no heart at that moment, for it would have beat loud and fast from terror. But being only tin, the Woodman was not at all afraid, although he was much disappointed.

"I am Oz, the Great and Terrible," spoke the Beast, in a voice that was one great roar. "Who are you, and why do you seek me?"

"I am a Woodman, and made of tin. Therefore I have no heart, and cannot love. I pray you to give me a heart that I may be as other men are."

"Why should I do this?" demanded the Beast.

"Because I ask it, and you alone can grant my request," answered the Woodman.

Oz gave a low growl at this, but said, gruffly: "If you indeed desire a heart, you must earn it."

"How?" asked the Woodman.

"Help Dorothy to kill the Wicked Witch of the West," replied the Beast. "When the Witch is dead, come to me, and I will then give you the biggest and kindest and most loving heart in all the Land of Oz."

So the Tin Woodman was forced to return sorrowfully to his friends and tell them of the terrible Beast he had seen. They all wondered greatly at the many forms the Great Wizard could take upon himself, and the Lion said:

"If he is a Beast when I go to see him, I shall roar my loudest, and so frighten him that he will grant all I ask. And if he is the lovely Lady, I shall pretend to spring upon her, and so compel her to do my bidding. And if he is the great Head, he will be at my mercy; for I will roll this head all about the room until he promises to give us what we desire. So be of good cheer, my friends, for all will yet be well."

The next morning the soldier with the green whiskers led the Lion to the great Throne Room and bade him enter the presence of Oz.

The Lion at once passed through the door, and glancing around saw, to his surprise, that before the throne was a Ball of Fire, so fierce and glowing he could scarcely bear to gaze upon it. His first thought was that Oz had by accident caught on fire and was burning up; but when he tried to go nearer, the heat was so intense that it singed his whiskers, and he crept back tremblingly to a spot nearer the door.

Then a low, quiet voice came from the Ball of Fire, and these were the words it spoke:

"I am Oz, the Great and Terrible. Who are you, and why do you seek me?"

And the Lion answered, "I am a Cowardly Lion, afraid of everything. I came to you to beg that you give me courage, so that in reality I may become the King of Beasts, as men call me."

"Why should I give you courage?" demanded Oz.

"Because of all Wizards you are the greatest, and alone have power to grant my request," answered the Lion.

The Ball of Fire burned fiercely for a time, and the voice said, "Bring me proof that the Wicked Witch is dead, and that moment I will give you courage. But as long as the Witch lives, you must remain a coward."

The Lion was angry at this speech, but could say nothing in reply, and while he stood silently gazing at the Ball of Fire it became so furiously hot that he turned tail and rushed from the room. He was glad to find his friends waiting for him, and told them of his terrible interview with the Wizard.

"What shall we do now?" asked Dorothy sadly.

"There is only one thing we can do," returned the Lion, "and that is to go to the land of the Winkies, seek out the Wicked Witch, and destroy her."

"But suppose we cannot?" said the girl.

"Then I shall never have courage," declared the Lion.

"And I shall never have brains," added the Scarecrow.

"And I shall never have a heart," spoke the Tin of Woodman.

"Oh, I don't like this Wizard's demands," said Dorothy, beginning to cry.

"Be careful!" cried the green girl. "The tears will fall on your green silk gown and spot it."

So Dorothy dried her eyes and said, "I suppose we must try it; but I am sure I do not want to kill anybody, even to see Aunt Em again."

"I will go with you; but I'm too much of a coward to kill the Witch," said the Lion.

"I will go too," declared the Scarecrow; "but I shall not be of much help to you, I am such a fool."

"I haven't the heart to harm even a Witch," remarked the Tin Woodman; "but if you go I certainly shall go with you."

Therefore it was decided to start upon their journey the next morning, and the Woodman sharpened his axe on a green grindstone and had all his joints properly oiled. The Scarecrow stuffed himself with fresh straw and Dorothy put new paint on his eyes that he might see better. The green girl, who was very kind to them, filled Dorothy's basket with good things to eat, and fastened a little bell around Toto's neck with a green ribbon.

They went to bed quite early and slept soundly until daylight, when they were awakened by the crowing of a green cock that lived in the back yard of the Palace, and the cackling of a hen that had laid a green egg.

12

The Search for
the Wicked Witch

T HE SOLDIER WITH the green whiskers led them through the streets
of the Emerald City until they reached the room where the Guardian of
the Gates lived. This officer unlocked their spectacles to put them back
in his great box, and then he politely opened the gate for our friends.

"Which road leads to the Wicked Witch of the West?" asked
Dorothy, shouldering her magical blue and silver gun.

"There is no road," answered the Guardian of the Gates. "No one
ever wishes to go that way."

"How, then, are we to find her?" inquired the girl.

"That will be easy," replied the man, "for when she knows you are in
the country of the Winkies she will find you, and make you all her
slaves."

"Perhaps not," said the Scarecrow, "for we mean to destroy her."

"Oh, that is different," said the Guardian of the Gates. "No one has
ever destroyed her before, so I naturally thought she would make slaves
of you, as she has of the rest. But take care; for she is wicked and fierce,
and may not allow you to destroy her. Keep to the West, where the sun
sets, and you cannot fail to find her."

They thanked him and bade him good-bye, and turned toward the
West, walking over fields of soft grass dotted here and there with daisies
and buttercups. Dorothy still wore the pretty silk dress she had put on in
the palace, but now, to her surprise, she found it was no longer green,
but pure white. The ribbon around Toto's neck had also lost its green
color and was as white as Dorothy's dress.

The Emerald City was soon left far behind. As they advanced the
ground became rougher and hillier, for there were no farms nor houses
in this country of the West, and the ground was untilled.

In the afternoon the sun shone hot in their faces, for there were no trees to offer them shade; so that before night Dorothy and Toto and the Lion were tired, and lay down upon the grass and fell asleep, with the Woodman and the Scarecrow keeping watch for anything interested in their brains.

Now the Wicked Witch of the West had but one eye, yet that was as powerful as a telescope, and could see everywhere. So, as she sat in the door of her castle, she happened to look around and saw Dorothy lying asleep, with her friends all about her. They were a long distance off, but the Wicked Witch was angry to find them in her country; so she blew upon a silver whistle that hung around her neck.

At once there came running to her from all directions a pack of great wolves. They had long legs and fierce eyes and sharp teeth.

"Go to those people," said the Witch, "and tear them to pieces."

"Are you not going to make them your slaves?" asked the leader of the wolves.

"No," she answered, "one is of tin, and one of straw; one is a girl and another a Lion. None of them is fit to work, so you may tear them into small pieces."

"Very well," said the wolf, and he dashed away at full speed, followed by the others.

It was lucky the Scarecrow and the Woodman were wide awake and heard the wolves coming.

"This is my fight," said the Woodman, "so get behind me and I will meet them as they come."

He seized his axe, which he had made very sharp, and as the leader of the wolves came on the Tin Woodman swung his arm and chopped the wolf's head from its body, so that it immediately died. As soon as he could raise his axe another wolf came up, and it also fell under the sharp edge of the Tin Woodman's weapon. There were forty wolves, and forty times a wolf was killed.

Soon, there was nothing but a heap of wolf parts on the ground. Severed snouts and heads and tails and feet. The grass was stained bright red and flies began to light on the chunks of meat. The air smelled of offal and made them wrinkle their noses, but they remained where they were, for they did not want to disturb Dorothy, who was still sleeping.

The Tin Woodman he put down his axe and sat beside the Scarecrow, who said, "It was a good fight, friend."

They waited until Dorothy awoke the next morning. The little girl was quite frightened when she saw the great pile of shaggy wolves, but the Tin Woodman told her all. She thanked him for saving them and sat down to breakfast, after which they started again upon their journey.

Now this same morning the Wicked Witch came to the door of her castle and looked out with her one eye that could see far off. She saw all her wolves lying dead, and the strangers still traveling through her country. "Unbelievable. How stupid is a wolf? What do they think? 'Hey, that guy with the axe is cutting everyone's head off. Perhaps I should run up to him as well. I wouldn't want to, oh, I don't know, maybe circle behind and take him by surprise. Or here's an idea, there's forty of us, let's make sure NOT to swarm him at once. No no, let's just keep running in a line toward the axe.'"

This rant made her angrier than before, and she blew her silver whistle twice.

Straightway a great flock of wild crows came flying toward her, enough to darken the sky.

And the Wicked Witch said to the King Crow, "Fly at once to the strangers; peck out their eyes and tear them to pieces."

The wild crows flew in one great flock toward Dorothy and her companions. When the little girl saw them coming she was afraid.

But the Scarecrow said, "This is my battle, so lie down beside me and you will not be harmed."

So they all lay upon the ground except the Scarecrow, and he stood up and stretched out his arms. And when the crows saw him they were frightened, as these birds always are by scarecrows, and did not dare to come any nearer. But the King Crow said:

"It is only a stuffed man. I will peck his eyes out."

The King Crow flew at the Scarecrow, who caught it by the head and twisted its neck until it died. And then another crow flew at him, and the Scarecrow twisted its neck also. There were forty crows, and forty times the Scarecrow twisted a neck, until at last all were lying dead beside him. Then he called to his companions to rise, and again they went upon their journey. Eventually the birds returned from death, but as all their necks were broken, they were merely one big flapping heap of brain-hungry feathers in the middle of nowhere.

When the Wicked Witch looked out again and saw all her crows flapping in a bloody heap, she got into a terrible rage. "Seriously? They did the same thing as the wolves? Perhaps something with less brains is the key." She blew three times upon her silver whistle.

Forthwith there was heard a great buzzing in the air, and a swarm of black bees came flying toward her.

"Go to the strangers and sting them to death!" commanded the

Witch, and the bees turned and flew rapidly until they came to where Dorothy and her friends were walking. But the Woodman had seen them coming, and the Scarecrow had decided what to do.

"Take out my straw and scatter it over the little girl and the dog and the Lion," he said to the Woodman, "and the bees cannot sting them." This the Woodman did, and as Dorothy lay close beside the Lion and held Toto in her arms, the straw covered them entirely.

The bees came and found no one but the Woodman to sting, so they flew at him and broke off all their stings against the tin, without hurting the Woodman at all. And as bees cannot live when their stings are broken that was the end of the black bees, and they lay scattered thick about the Woodman, like little heaps of fine coal.

Then Dorothy and the Lion got up, and the girl helped the Tin Woodman put the straw back into the Scarecrow again, until he was as good as ever. So they started upon their journey once more.

The Wicked Witch was so angry when she saw her black bees in little heaps like fine coal that she stamped her foot and tore her hair and gnashed her teeth. And then she called a dozen of her slaves, who were the Winkies, and gave them sharp spears, telling them to go to the strangers and destroy them.

The Winkies were not a brave people, but they had to do as they were told. So they marched away until they came near to Dorothy. Then the Lion gave a great roar and sprang toward them, and the poor Winkies were so frightened that they ran back as fast as they could.

When they returned to the castle the Wicked Witch beat them well with a strap, and sent them back to their work, after which she sat down to think what she should do next. She could not understand how all her plans to destroy these strangers had failed; but she was a powerful Witch, as well as a wicked one, and she soon made up her mind how to act.

There was, in her cupboard, a Golden Cap, with a circle of diamonds and rubies running round it. This Golden Cap had a charm. Whoever owned it could call three times upon the Winged Monkeys, who would obey any order they were given. But no person could command these strange creatures more than three times. Twice already the Wicked Witch had used the charm of the Cap. Once was when she had made the Winkies her slaves, and set herself to rule over their country. The Winged Monkeys had helped her do this. The second time was when she had fought against the Great Oz himself, and driven him out of the land of the West. The Winged Monkeys had also helped her in doing this. Only once more could she use this Golden Cap, for which reason she did not like to do so until all her other powers were exhausted. But now that her fierce wolves and her wild crows and her stinging bees were gone, and her slaves had been scared away by the Cowardly Lion, she saw there was only one way left to destroy Dorothy and her friends.

So the Wicked Witch took the Golden Cap from her cupboard and placed it upon her head. Then she stood upon her left foot and said slowly:

"Ep-pe, pep-pe, kak-ke!"

Next she stood upon her right foot and said:

"Hil-lo, hol-lo, hel-lo!"

After this she stood upon both feet and cried in a loud voice:

"Ziz-zy, zuz-zy, zik!"

Now the charm began to work. The sky was darkened, and a low rumbling sound was heard in the air. There was a rushing of many wings, a great chattering and laughing, and the sun came out of the dark sky to show the Wicked Witch surrounded by a crowd of monkeys, each with a pair of immense and powerful wings on his shoulders.

One, much bigger than the others, seemed to be their leader. He flew close to the Witch and said, "You have called us for the third and last time. What do you command?"

"Go to the strangers who are within my land and destroy them all except the Lion," said the Wicked Witch. "Bring that beast to me, for I have a mind to harness him like a horse, and make him work."

"Your commands shall be obeyed," said the leader. Then, with a great deal of chattering and noise, the Winged Monkeys flew away to the place where Dorothy and her friends were walking.

Some of the Monkeys seized the Tin Woodman and carried him through the air until they were over a country thickly covered with sharp rocks. Here they dropped the poor Woodman, who fell a great distance to the rocks, where he lay so battered and dented that he could neither move nor groan.

Others of the Monkeys caught the Scarecrow, and with their long fingers pulled all of the straw out of his clothes and head. They made his hat and boots and clothes into a small bundle and threw it into the top branches of a tall tree.

The remaining Monkeys threw pieces of stout rope around the Lion and wound many coils about his body and head and legs, until he was unable to bite or scratch or struggle in any way. Then they lifted him up and flew away with him to the Witch's castle, where he was placed in a small yard with a high iron fence around it, so that he could not escape.

But Dorothy they did not harm at all. She stood, with Toto in her arms, watching the sad fate of her comrades and thinking it would soon be her turn. The leader of the Winged Monkeys flew up to her, his long, hairy arms stretched out and his ugly face grinning terribly; but he saw the mark of the Good Witch's kiss upon her forehead and stopped short, motioning the others not to touch her.

"We dare not harm this little girl," he said to them, "for she is protected by the Power of Good, and that is greater than the Power of Evil."

"Is that true?" one of the monkeys whispered to his friend.

"I don't know," replied the friend, "I think he just makes stuff up as he sees fit."

"All we can do is to carry her to the castle of the Wicked Witch and leave her there," continued leader of the Winged Monkeys.

So, carefully and gently, they lifted Dorothy in their arms and carried her swiftly through the air until they came to the castle, where they set her down upon the front doorstep. Then the leader said to the Witch:

"We have obeyed you as far as we were able. The Tin Woodman and the Scarecrow are destroyed, and the Lion is tied up in your yard. The little girl we dare not harm, nor the dog she carries in her arms. Your power over our band is now ended, and you will never see us again."

"Pity, I so loved it when you tried to pick lice out of my hair. Whatever shall I do without your preening skills?"

"I sense sarcasm," said the leader.

"Give the monkey a banana."

"If you're looking for a fight—"

The Witch cut him off with a bolt of fire from her hand. All the Winged Monkeys screamed, and with much chattering and noise, flew into the air and were soon out of sight.

The Wicked Witch was both surprised and worried when she saw the mark on Dorothy's forehead, for she knew well that neither the Winged Monkeys nor she, herself, dare hurt the girl in any way. She looked down at Dorothy's feet, and seeing the Silver Shoes covered in goops of blood, began to tremble with fear, for she knew what a powerful charm belonged to them. Then she saw the rifle, and knew its magic was deadly. At first the Witch was tempted to run away from Dorothy; but she happened to look into the child's eyes and saw how simple the soul behind them was, and that the little girl did not know of the wonderful power the Silver Shoes gave her. So the Wicked Witch laughed to herself, and thought, "I can still make her my slave, for she does not know how to use her power."

Then she took the gun away and said to Dorothy, harshly and severely:

"Come with me; and see that you mind everything I tell you, for if you do not I will make an end of you, as I did of the Tin Woodman and the Scarecrow."

Dorothy followed her through many of the beautiful rooms in her castle until they came to the kitchen, where the Witch bade her clean the pots and kettles and sweep the floor.

Dorothy went to work meekly, with her mind made up to work as hard as she could; for she was glad the Wicked Witch had decided not to kill her. But it was frightening to work in the Witch's castle, for many of her slaves were the undead. Undead Winkies, undead Munchkins, even undead humans, whom Dorothy assumed had been farmers at some point. The Witch kept these creatures on short chains, and hung extracted brains in front of them on hooks. As they reached for the brains, they would pull on their chains, which in turn activated many levers that performed various functions: opening and closing doors, stoking fires, stirring potions in large cauldrons, feeding her collection of wild animals she kept in cages. Dorothy skirted wide of these abominations, for whenever they saw her they turned their attention to her and tried to grab her. Their yellow teeth clicked in anticipation for her fresh brains.

As Dorothy was retrieving a broom from a small closest, she watched one of these undead humans reaching for the brains in front of it. As it did, a tiny gun slid out from a hole in the wall and shot a bullet into one of the undead creatures on the other side of the room. Its brains splattered all over Dorothy, and all over the floor she had been cleaning. The creature fell motionless, swaying on its own chain.

"Why, she just uses them for amusement," Dorothy lamented. "That is just sick. How will I ever keep the floors clean if they are constantly awash in skull and brain?"

With Dorothy hard at work, the Witch thought she would go into the courtyard and harness the Cowardly Lion like a horse; it would amuse her, she was sure, to make him draw her chariot whenever she wished to go to drive. But as she opened the gate the Lion gave a loud roar and bounded at her so fiercely that the Witch was afraid, and ran out and shut the gate again.

"If I cannot harness you," said the Witch to the Lion, speaking through the bars of the gate, "I can starve you. You shall have nothing to eat until you do as I wish."

So after that she took no food to the imprisoned Lion; but every day she came to the gate at noon and asked, "Are you ready to be harnessed like a horse?"

And the Lion would answer, "No. If you come in this yard, I will bite you."

The reason the Lion did not have to do as the Witch wished was that every night, while the woman was asleep, Dorothy carried him bits of gray meat that she cleaned up off the floor. She did not tell the Lion where the meat originally came from, for it was better he eat the guts of the undead than starve to death.

After he had eaten he would lie down on his bed of straw, and Dorothy would lie beside him and put her head on his soft, shaggy mane, while they talked of better times. They would listen to the moaning of the hungry undead chained to the walls inside and wonder if this land would ever be free from the plague, even if they did kill the Witch. First they needed to escape, they realized, but they could find no way to get out of the castle, for it was constantly guarded by the yellow Winkies, the undead, and many wild animals, all of whom who were the slaves of the Wicked Witch and too afraid of her not to do as she told them.

The girl had to work hard during the day, and often the Witch threatened to beat her with the same old umbrella she always carried in her hand. But, in truth, she did not dare to strike Dorothy, because of the mark upon her forehead. The child did not know this, and was full of fear for herself and Toto. Once the Witch struck Toto a blow with her umbrella and the brave little dog flew at her and bit her leg in return. The Witch did not bleed where she was bitten, for she was so wicked that the blood in her had dried up many years before.

Dorothy's life became very sad as she grew to understand that it would be harder than ever to get back to Kansas and Aunt Em again. She no longer cared about her promise to the Good Witch. This land could rot for all she cared. She didn't belong here and she didn't want to be burdened with its problems. Sometimes she would cry bitterly for hours, with Toto sitting at her feet and looking into her face, whining dismally to show how sorry he was for his little mistress. Toto did not really care whether he was in Kansas or the Land of Oz so long as Dorothy was with him; but he knew the little girl was unhappy, and that made him unhappy too.

Now the Wicked Witch had a great longing to have for her own the Silver Shoes which the girl always wore. Her bees and her crows and her wolves were lying in heaps and drying up, and she had used up all the power of the Golden Cap; but if she could only get hold of the Silver Shoes, they would give her more power than all the other things she had lost. She watched Dorothy carefully, to see if she ever took off her shoes, thinking she might steal them. But the child was so proud of her pretty shoes that she never took them off except at night and when she took her bath. The Witch was too much afraid of the dark to dare go in Dorothy's room at night to take the shoes, and her dread of water was greater than her fear of the dark, so she never came near when Dorothy was bathing. Indeed, the old Witch never touched water, nor ever let water touch her in any way. Because of this she smelled so foul most people could not tell her scent from that of all the undead around her.

But the wicked creature was very cunning, and she finally thought of a trick that would give her what she wanted. She made some of the chains on her undead slaves longer than normal, so that when Dorothy walked across the floor she was suddenly grasped by decaying, rotted hands. As she struggled to free herself, kicking and punching at the disgusting creatures, one of her Silver Shoes came off; and before she could reach it, the Witch had snatched it away and put it on her own skinny foot.

The wicked woman was greatly pleased with the success of her trick, for as long as she had one of the shoes she owned half the power of their charm, and Dorothy could not use it against her, even had she known how to do so. She then jammed her umbrella into the eye of the undead Winkie grasping Dorothy, and let the monster's blood ooze down over the little girl's hair.

The little girl rolled free from the creature's hands, and seeing she had lost one of her pretty shoes, grew angry. She said to the Witch, "Give me back my shoe!"

"I will not," retorted the Witch, "for it is now my shoe, and not yours."

"You are a wicked creature!" cried Dorothy. "You have no right to take my shoe from me."

"I shall keep it, just the same," said the Witch, laughing at her, "and someday I shall get the other one from you, too."

This made Dorothy so very angry that she punched the Witch in the nose.

In turn the Witch hit Dorothy on the head with the umbrella. The poor little girl saw stars in front of her eyes and stumbled over to the pantry to steady herself on the door knob, but when she grabbed it the door opened. Inside, Dorothy saw the magic rifle leaning against the shelves that were stocked with potion ingredients. Quickly, she raced inside and snatched it up.

"Leave that gun alone, child," the Witch commanded.

"NO! I am tired of you keeping me as a slave. You have ruined this land with monsters and curses and I want to go home."

The Witch sighed. "I need better help. Which one of my idiot minions put the gun in there? I told them to have it destroyed. So what are you going to do, shoot me? You are just a child and do not know how to hurt anyone."

"I will not shoot you," cried Dorothy, raising the gun and aiming it at the Witch's head, "but I will make you a deal. If you end your evil ways and put a stop to these awful dead things that keep eating everyone's brains, I will simply tell the Great Wizard you are dead and leave you in peace."

"The Great Wizard put you up to this?"

"He says he can't fix the mess you've made if you're still alive."

"I should have known. No one comes out to my part of the land without nefarious intents. Well, I'll have to pay him a visit. Perhaps it's time the Emerald City has a taste of its own brains."

This made Dorothy even angrier, for she knew that if the Witch's curse were to do its work on the people of the Emerald City, that it might stop her from seeing Oz again. Then she would never get home. "If you do that I will surely shoot you."

"Oh come on now, child, you are not going to shoot anyone."

Dorothy spun around and shot one of the undead Munchkins chained to the wall. Its head exploded and the body fell to the ground.

"Big deal," said the Witch, wiping the Munchkin's brains off her face. "It was already dead."

She licked some of the fresh blood off her hands and swallowed it with a smile.

Dorothy re-cocked the gun. "The next one goes into your head." At her feet, Toto barked to tell her it was a good idea.

"Not before I can blast you with fire, burning you alive."

"Try me, Witch."

But the Witch did not shoot fire from her hands. Instead she simply mumbled the words, "Biffy, hiffy, tiffy," and suddenly all the chains on all of the undead in the castle came undone.

Dorothy saw all of the undead Winkies and Munchkins and humans now shambling toward her, and she realized that she would never get out of the castle.

"You shouldn't mess with me," the Witch said. "I am much more powerful than—"

Bang! Dorothy fired the gun. The bullet whizzed by the Witch's head and disappeared.

"You missed, child. Now it's my turn." The Witch raised her hand to shoot fire, but the bullet came back and scalped her, taking her hat and hair clean off and splattering it against a nearby stove. The Witch cried in pain and fell to her knees.

"Come on, Toto, it's time to get out of here." Dorothy snatched the Silver Shoe off of the Witch and dodged two undead Winkies reaching for her. She and the little dog weaved through many of the creatures until they found a staircase going up. Behind her, many shambling Munchkins were following, moaning, "Braiiiins." Dorothy fired another round and ran up the stairs. The bullet elongated in midair until it was as thin and flat as a blade and cut off the heads of the Munchkins.

On the kitchen floor the Witch rose, and put her hand to her head. Trembling, she cursed as she felt the soft ridges of her own black brain. She would have chanted a spell to bring Dorothy back to her so she could torture the little girl, but she never had the chance, for a collection of her own undead slaves swarmed her and wrestled her to the ground. They dug their teeth into her brain and pulled out ridge upon ridge of her gray matter. When they were done with her brains, they began eating her face and neck, then her arms and chest, then her legs, until there was nothing left of the Witch but bloody bones.

Upstairs, Dorothy found herself surrounded by more liberated undead slaves. She fired the gun and the bullet grew to the size of a tractor tire and then exploded in midair, sending bits of shrapnel into the heads of her attackers.

She soon found herself high up on one of the castle's turrets. Looking down she could see into the Lion's pen far below. He was still chained up and many of the undead were circling around him. The Lion was quick and snapped his mighty jaws at the creatures, knocking them back. "Stand clear," yelled Dorothy. The Lion looked up and saw her and knew she would save him. He backed away and huddled against the wall. Dorothy fired her gun. The bullet turned to hot oil in midair and showered all of the undead, melting them to puddles of blood and bone.

"Hurry and free me," he Lion shouted. "There are more coming."

Dorothy scooped up Toto in her arms and yelled back, "I am too high to jump. I will be splattered."

"I will catch you, I promise."

So Dorothy held her breath and leapt off the turret, holding Toto in her arm. She fell very fast and thought surely she would meet her end on the ground below. But the Lion was true to his word and leapt up, catching her on his back in midair, and landing gracefully on the ground.

"Shoot my chains," he said.

Dorothy shot the chains and set him free and together they raced out of the pen.

Everywhere the undead were coming for them. Many of the living Winkies who had been serving as slaves were busy fighting for their lives. The sounds of teeth chewing apart flesh resounded off the castle walls. Dorothy wanted to help them but knew that even with her magical gun she was outnumbered. Before she and the Lion raced out of the castle grounds she yelled very loudly to anyone who could hear her, "If you make it out meet us by the pile of wolves!"

13

The Rendezvous

A DAY LATER DOROTHY, the Cowardly Lion, and several blood-stained Winkies were standing by the wolf carcasses left by the Tin Woodman. Both Dorothy and the Lion were much pleased to hear that the Wicked Witch had been eaten alive. The only downside to her death was that now there were many undead roaming freely around the castle, even more than before.

There was great rejoicing among the yellow Winkies that had escaped, for they had been made to work hard during many years for the Wicked Witch, who had always treated them with great cruelty. They kept this day as a holiday, then and ever after, and spent the time in feasting and dancing.

"If our friends, the Scarecrow and the Tin Woodman, were only with us," said the Lion, "I should be quite happy."

"Don't you suppose we could rescue them?" asked the girl anxiously.

"We can try," answered the Lion.

So they called the yellow Winkies and asked them if they would help to rescue their friends, and the Winkies said that they would be delighted to do all in their power for Dorothy, who had set them free from bondage. So she chose a number of the Winkies who looked as if they knew the most, and they all started away. They traveled that day and part of the next until they came to the rocky plain where the Tin Woodman lay, all battered and bent. His axe was near him, but the blade was rusted and the handle broken off short.

The Winkies lifted him tenderly in their arms, and carried him to the nearest Winkie Village, Dorothy shedding a few tears by the way at the sad plight of her old friend, and the Lion looking sober and sorry. When they reached the village Dorothy said to the Winkies:

"Are any of your people tinsmiths?"

"Oh, yes. Some of us are very good tinsmiths," they told her.

"Then bring them to me," she said. And when the tinsmiths came, bringing with them all their tools in baskets, she inquired, "Can you straighten out those dents in the Tin Woodman, and bend him back into shape again, and solder him together where he is broken?"

The tinsmiths looked the Woodman over carefully and then answered that they thought they could mend him so he would be as good as ever. So they set to work in one of the big yellow houses and worked for three days and four nights, hammering and twisting and bending and soldering and polishing and pounding at the legs and body and head of the Tin Woodman, until at last he was straightened out into his old form, and his joints worked as well as ever. To be sure, there were several patches on him, but the tinsmiths did a good job, and as the Woodman was not a vain man he did not mind the patches at all.

When, at last, he walked into Dorothy's room and thanked her for rescuing him, he was so pleased that he wept tears of joy, and Dorothy had to wipe every tear carefully from his face with her apron, so his joints would not be rusted. At the same time her own tears fell thick and fast at the joy of meeting her old friend again, and these tears did not need to be wiped away. As for the Lion, he wiped his eyes so often with the tip of his tail that it became quite wet, and he was obliged to go out into the courtyard and hold it in the sun till it dried.

"If we only had the Scarecrow with us again," said the in Woodman, when Dorothy had finished telling him everything that had happened, "I should be quite happy."

"We must try to find him," said the girl.

So she called the Winkies to help her, and they walked all that day and part of the next until they came to the tall tree in the branches of which the Winged Monkeys had tossed the Scarecrow's clothes.

It was a very tall tree, and the trunk was so smooth that no one could climb it; but the Woodman said at once, "I'll chop it down, and then we can get the Scarecrow's clothes."

Now while the tinsmiths had been at work mending the Woodman himself, another of the Winkies, who was a goldsmith, had made an axe-handle of solid gold and fitted it to the Woodman's axe, instead of the old broken handle. Others polished the blade until all the rust was removed and it glistened like burnished silver.

As soon as he had spoken, the Tin Woodman began to chop, and in a short time the tree fell over with a crash, whereupon the Scarecrow's clothes fell out of the branches and rolled off on the ground.

Dorothy picked them up and had the Winkies carry them back to the village, where they were stuffed with nice, clean straw; and behold! here was the Scarecrow, as good as ever, thanking them over and over again for saving him.

Now that they were reunited, Dorothy and her friends spent a few happy days at the Yellow Village, where they found everything they needed to make them comfortable.

But soon the undead began to show up, having found their way from the castle. The Winkies had plenty of rifles, and the battle was over fairly quickly. Now, brains and blood stained most of the yellow houses. This reminded Dorothy they needed to get back to Oz. "We must go back, and claim his promise."

"Yes," said the Woodman, "at last I shall get my heart."

"And I shall get my brains," added the Scarecrow joyfully.

"And I shall get my courage," said the Lion thoughtfully.

"And I shall get back to Kansas," cried Dorothy, clapping her hands. "Oh, let us start for the Emerald City tomorrow!"

This they decided to do. The next day they called the Winkies together and bade them good-bye. The Winkies were sorry to have them go, and they had grown so fond of the Tin Woodman that they begged him to stay and rule over them and the Yellow Land of the West. Finding they were determined to go, the Winkies gave Toto and the Lion each a golden collar; and to Dorothy they presented a beautiful bracelet studded with diamonds; and to the Scarecrow they gave a gold-headed walking stick, to keep him from stumbling; and to the Tin Woodman they offered a silver oil-can, inlaid with gold and set with precious jewels. The Winkies even gave them rifles and plenty of ammunition.

Every one of the travelers shook hands with them until their arms ached.

Before they left there was one last present for Dorothy. One of the Winkies who had escaped the castle had filched the Golden Cap on his way out. He gave it to Dorothy, explaining he did not need its powers, but that she probably would. She tried it on her own head and found that it fitted her exactly. She did not know exactly what the Golden Cap's power was, for the Winkie did not explain it, but she saw that it was pretty, so she made up her mind to wear it and carry her sunbonnet in the basket.

Then, being prepared for the journey, they all started for the Emerald City; and the Winkies gave them three cheers and many good wishes to carry with them.

14

The Battle of the Winged Monkeys

YOU WILL REMEMBER there was no road—not even a pathway—between the castle of the Wicked Witch and the Emerald City. When the four travelers went in search of the Witch she had seen them coming, and so sent the Winged Monkeys to bring them to her. It was much harder to find their way back through the big fields of buttercups and yellow daisies than it was being carried. They knew, of course, they must go straight east, toward the rising sun; and they started off in the right way. But at noon, when the sun was over their heads, they did not know which was east and which was west, and that was the reason they were lost in the great fields. They kept on walking, however, and at night the moon came out and shone brightly. So they lay down among the sweet smelling yellow flowers and slept soundly until morning—all but the Scarecrow and the Tin Woodman.

The next morning the sun was behind a cloud, but they started on, as if they were quite sure which way they were going.

"If we walk far enough," said Dorothy, "I am sure we shall sometime come to some place."

But day by day passed away, and they still saw nothing before them but the scarlet fields. The Scarecrow began to grumble a bit.

"We have surely lost our way," he said, "and unless we find it again in time to reach the Emerald City, I shall never get my brains."

"Nor I my heart," declared the Tin Woodman. "It seems to me I can scarcely wait till I get to Oz, and you must admit this is a very long journey."

"You see," said the Cowardly Lion, with a whimper, "I haven't the courage to keep tramping forever, without getting anywhere at all."

Then Dorothy lost heart. She sat down on the grass and looked at her companions, and they sat down and looked at her, and Toto found that for the first time in his life he was too tired to chase a butterfly that flew past his head. So he put out his tongue and panted and looked at Dorothy as if to ask what they should do next.

"Suppose we call the field mice," she suggested. "They could probably tell us the way to the Emerald City."

"To be sure they could," cried the Scarecrow, "if they are still alive. For all we know they are eating brains now."

"It is worth a shot," said the Lion.

Dorothy blew the little whistle she had always carried about in her pocket since the Queen of the Field Mice had given it to her. In a few minutes they heard the pattering of tiny feet, and many of the small gray mice came running up to her. Among them was the Queen herself. One of her legs was in a tiny bandage, and she was battle-scarred from her last fight. She asked, in her squeaky little voice:

"What can I do for my friends?"

"We have lost our way," said Dorothy. "Can you tell us where the Emerald City is?"

"Certainly," answered the Queen; "but it is a great way off, for you have had it at your backs all this time." Then she noticed Dorothy's Golden Cap, and said, "Why don't you use the charm of the Cap, and call the Winged Monkeys to you? They will carry you to the City of Oz in less than an hour."

"I didn't know there was a charm," answered Dorothy, in surprise. "What is it?"

"It is written inside the Golden Cap," replied the Queen of the Field Mice. "But if you are going to call the Winged Monkeys we must run away, for they are full of mischief and think it great fun to play with us."

"Won't they hurt me?" asked the girl anxiously.

"Oh, no. They must obey the wearer of the Cap. Good-bye!" And she scampered out of sight, with all the mice hurrying after her.

Dorothy looked inside the Golden Cap and saw some words written upon the lining. These, she thought, must be the charm, so she read the directions carefully and put the Cap upon her head.

"Ep-pe, pep-pe, kak-ke!" she said, standing on her left foot.

"What did you say?" asked the Scarecrow, who did not know what she was doing.

"Hil-lo, hol-lo, hel-lo!" Dorothy went on, standing this time on her right foot.

"Hello!" replied the Tin Woodman calmly.

"Ziz-zy, zuz-zy, zik!" said Dorothy, who was now standing on both feet. This ended the saying of the charm, and they heard a great chattering and flapping of wings, as the band of Winged Monkeys flew up to them.

The King bowed low before Dorothy, and asked, "What is your command?"

"We wish to go to the Emerald City," said the child, "and we have lost our way."

"We will carry you," replied the King, and no sooner had he spoken than two of the Monkeys caught Dorothy in their arms and flew away with her. Others took the Scarecrow and the Woodman and the Lion, and one little Monkey seized Toto and flew after them, although the dog tried hard to bite him.

The Scarecrow and the Tin Woodman were rather frightened at first, for they remembered how badly the Winged Monkeys had treated them before; but they saw that no harm was intended, so they rode through the air quite cheerfully, and had a fine time looking at the pretty gardens and woods far below them.

Dorothy found herself riding easily between two of the biggest Monkeys, one of them the King himself. They had made a chair of their hands and were careful not to hurt her.

"Why do you have to obey the charm of the Golden Cap?" she asked.

"That is a long story," answered the King, with a Winged laugh; "but as we have a long journey before us, I will pass the time by telling you about it, if you wish."

"I shall be glad to hear it," she replied.

"Once," began the leader, "we were a free people, living happily in the great forest, flying from tree to tree, eating nuts and fruit and doing just as we pleased without calling anybody master. Perhaps some of us were rather too full of mischief at times, flying down to pull the tails of the animals that had no wings, chasing birds, and throwing nuts at the people who walked in the forest. But we were careless and happy and full of fun, and enjoyed every minute of the day. This was many years ago, long before Oz came out of the clouds to rule over this land.

"There lived here then, away at the North, a beautiful princess, who was also a powerful sorceress. All her magic was used to help the people, and she was never known to hurt anyone who was good. Her name was Gayelette, and she lived in a handsome palace built from great blocks of ruby. Everyone loved her, but her greatest sorrow was that she could find no one to love in return, since all the men were much too stupid and ugly to mate with one so beautiful and wise. At last, however, she found a boy who was handsome and manly and wise beyond his years. Gayelette made up her mind that when he grew to be a man she would make him her husband, so she took him to her ruby palace and used all her magic powers to make him as strong and good and lovely as any woman could wish. When he grew to manhood, Quelala, as he was called, was said to be the best and wisest man in all the land, while his manly beauty was so great that Gayelette loved him dearly, and hastened to make everything ready for the wedding.

"My grandfather was at that time the King of the Winged Monkeys which lived in the forest near Gayelette's palace, and the old fellow loved a joke better than a good dinner. One day, just before the wedding, my grandfather was flying out with his band when he saw Quelala walking beside the river. He was dressed in a rich costume of pink silk and purple velvet, and my grandfather thought he would see what he could do. At his word the band flew down and seized Quelala, carried him in their arms until they were over the middle of the river, and then dropped him into the water.

"'Swim out, my fine fellow,' cried my grandfather, 'and see if the water has spotted your clothes.' Quelala was much too wise not to swim, and he was not in the least spoiled by all his good fortune. He laughed, when he came to the top of the water, and swam in to shore. But when Gayelette came running out to him she found his silks and velvet all ruined by the river.

"The princess was angry, and she knew, of course, who did it. She had all the Winged Monkeys brought before her, and she said at first that their wings should be tied and they should be treated as they had treated Quelala, and dropped in the river. But my grandfather pleaded hard, for he knew the Monkeys would drown in the river with their wings tied, and Quelala said a kind word for them also; so that Gayelette finally spared them, on condition that the Winged Monkeys should ever after do three times the bidding of the owner of the Golden Cap. This Cap had been made for a wedding present to Quelala, and it is said to have cost the princess half her kingdom. Of course my grandfather and all the other Monkeys at once agreed to the condition, and that is how it happens that we are three times the slaves of the owner of the Golden Cap, whosoever he may be."

"And what became of them?" asked Dorothy, who had been greatly interested in the story.

"Quelala being the first owner of the Golden Cap," replied the

Monkey, "he was the first to lay his wishes upon us. As his bride could not bear the sight of us, he called us all to him in the forest after he had married her and ordered us always to keep where she could never again set eyes on a Winged Monkey, which we were glad to do, for we were all afraid of her.

"This was all we ever had to do until the Golden Cap fell into the hands of the Wicked Witch of the West, who made us enslave the Winkies, and afterward drive Oz himself out of the Land of the West. Now the Golden Cap is yours, and three times you have the right to lay your wishes upon us."

As the Monkey King finished his story Dorothy looked toward the sun and saw a terrible sight. Wave upon wave of the beastly Stappers was flying their way.

"Look out!" she cried, as the huge flying monsters, each one part spider, part scorpion and part wasp zoomed in toward them.

From their dangling positions under the flying Monkeys, the Tin Woodman and the Scarecrow fired their newly acquired rifles at the attackers. Two Stappers fell from the sky with holes in their heads and crashed to the ground below, their bodies exploding on the rocks like rotten fruit.

"Quickly," the King yelled to his fellow Monkeys, "defensive positions. Take them out of the sky!"

The Monkeys swooped and dove, doing their best to avoid the massive stingers, hooked tails, and hairy legs of the Stappers. Dorothy prayed hard and held Toto tight as her escort banked out of the way of a black, giant stinger. The beast circled around but was intercepted by two other Monkeys. They kicked the flying beast in the side but its stinger and tail were too fast, and whipped about catching each Monkey in the belly. Its fast-acting poison made the Monkeys go still in the air, and it ate them both in one click of its mandibles.

More Monkeys dove in from overhead, forming a defensive wall behind Dorothy. She did her best to unsling her gun but her escort was busy dodging the Stappers coming in from the front, and it was all she could do to hang on.

She watched in horror as the Monkeys carrying the Lion were sideswiped, each one spinning off into the air to get eaten and stung by the flying insect monstrosities. The Lion roared as he fell, and one of the Stappers swooped in toward him, thrusting its stinger out for a kill. The Lion knocked the stinger away with his huge paws and bit the Stapper on the leg. This was a good thing since it stopped the Lion from falling to his death. He hung on as the flying beast ascended, flipping upside down and rolling over to get the Lion off of it. But the Lion held fast.

"Somebody get the Lion," the King yelled, banking once again to the side to avoid a slashing stinger.

The Stappers were also coming to the rescue of their cohort, honing in on the dangling Lion. But the Tin Woodman fired a shot and hit one of them in the back, tearing its wing off. The wounded Stapper began to fly uncontrollably in a circle and the Woodman shot it again, hitting it square in the middle of its many eyes. It fell in a heap to the ground.

But the Lion was still hanging precariously from the hairy leg, and trying desperately to dodge the multi-segmented tail lashing at it with its hooked, poisonous barb on the end.

"Get me closer," shouted the Scarecrow, "and I will save him." So the Monkey carrying the scarecrow flew in close, and the Scarecrow estimated the distance, for during his time on the pole in the farm field he was good at estimating how long crows in the distance would take to reach him. He fired his rifle and cheered as the segmented tail of the Stapper ripped from the monster's body and twirled to the ground. His next shot hit the beast in the neck and made it go still. It began to fall and Dorothy cried for someone to help, for surely the Lion would be dashed to bits on the ground below. But the Monkeys were prepared for this and caught the Lion in a four-way basket seat.

Of course they were not out of danger yet. Monkeys were falling from the sky left and right. And now a few dead Monkeys had flown back up into the air and were trying to eat the brains of everything besides the Scarecrow.

"There are too many of them," cried the King, "they will kill us and eat us. Even my old friends are trying to eat us now."

"I have an idea," said the Scarecrow. "Do you see those windmills in the distance. Fly us to them and stop just in front of them." So the Monkeys did this, carrying their wards, and flew to a low hill whereupon stood eight of the most magnificent windmills Dorothy had ever seen. Each one was made of solid gold, and their blades twirled softly in the breeze. She would have liked to see inside them, but the horrific buzzing behind her told her the Stappers were coming in for a kill. Sure enough, when she looked back, she saw a whole swarm of them speeding toward her and the Monkeys.

"Hold steady," cried the Scarecrow, "and when I say duck, everybody drop to the ground."

The Stappers came in fast, with a collection of undead Monkeys behind them. Half of the Stappers gave up their chase and turned back to fight the Monkeys, for they didn't care what they ate. In this land there was never enough food. They battled high up in the air, the Monkeys landing on the Stappers and biting their flesh, the Stappers stinging the Monkeys and eating them. The King cried with sorrow at what had become of his friends.

There were only six Stappers coming in now. They were almost on top of the travelers.

"Duck!"

The Monkeys dove for the ground, careful not to hurt their passengers. The Stappers, their tiny brains not ready for the maneuver, flew right into the blades of the windmills. The blades were not moving very fast but they were very heavy and the speed and momentum of the Stappers was enough that all six were cut in half. Heads and upper thoraxes went one way, legs, tails and stingers went another.

"What a perfect trick," Dorothy said to the Scarecrow. "I'm so glad you thought of it."

The rest of the Monkeys watched the battle taking place above them between the undead Monkeys and remaining Stappers. "What now?" asked the Monkey who was carrying the Tin Woodman.

"Now we must get to the Wizard," said Dorothy. "I fear your friends in the air are no longer your friends, and we must hurry and leave while both enemies are occupied with each other."

So the Monkeys once again lifted the travelers into the sky and flew toward the Emerald City. Soon they saw the green, shining walls of the city before them. She wondered at the rapid flight of the Monkeys, but was glad the journey was over. The Monkeys set the travelers down carefully before the gate of the City, the King bowed low to Dorothy, and then flew swiftly away, followed by all his band.

"That was a terrifying ride," said the little girl.

"Yes, but a quick way out of our troubles," replied the Lion, whose mouth was stained with Stapper blood. "How lucky it was you received that wonderful Cap!"

15

The Discovery of Oz,
the Terrible

THE FOUR TRAVELERS walked up to the great gate of Emerald City
and rang the bell. After ringing several times, it was opened by the same
Guardian of the Gates they had met before.

"Who are you?" he asked.

"What do you mean, 'who are we?'" the Lion replied. "It's us, the
four who went to kill the Witch."

Toto barked to inform the Lion there were five of them but the Lion
didn't speak dog so his point was lost.

"What! Are you back again?" the Guardian asked, in surprise.

"Do you not see us?" answered the Scarecrow.

"But . . . you don't look like you."

Dorothy looked at herself and her friends and understood what the
Guardian meant, for they were all covered in Stapper blood, and were
scratched and cut. They looked such a fright that she almost didn't
recognize herself. And to boot, they were each wielding guns now.

"Well it is us," said the Scarecrow.

"And the Witch let you go again?" asked the man, in wonder.

"She could not help it, for she is dead," explained the Scarecrow.

"Dead!"

"Eaten, to be exact."

"Eaten! Well, that is good news, indeed," said the man. "Who ate
her?" He was looking at the Lion, especially at the blood around his
mouth.

"It was the undead Winkies," said the Lion gravely. "But only
because Dorothy shot her."

"Good gracious!" exclaimed the man, and he bowed very low indeed
before her.

Then he led them into his little room and locked the spectacles from the great box on all their eyes, just as he had done before. Afterward they passed on through the gate into the Emerald City. When the people heard from the Guardian of the Gates that Dorothy had caused the death of the Wicked Witch of the West, they all gathered around the travelers and followed them in a great crowd to the Palace of Oz.

The soldier with the green whiskers was still on guard before the door, but he let them in at once, and they were again met by the beautiful green girl, who showed each of them to their old rooms at once, so they might rest until the Great Oz was ready to receive them.

The soldier had the news carried straight to Oz that Dorothy and the other travelers had come back again, after destroying the Wicked Witch; but Oz made no reply. They thought the Great Wizard would send for them at once, but he did not. They had no word from him the next day, nor the next, nor the next. The waiting was tiresome and wearing, but at least they were able clean themselves. At last they grew vexed that Oz should treat them in so poor a fashion, after sending them to undergo hardships and slavery. So the Scarecrow at last asked the green girl to take another message to Oz, saying if he did not let them in to see him at once they would call the Winged Monkeys to help them, and find out whether he kept his promises or not. When the Wizard was given this message he was so frightened that he sent word for them to come to the Throne Room at four minutes after nine o'clock the next morning. He had once met the Winged Monkeys in the Land of the West, and he did not wish to meet them again.

The four travelers passed a sleepless night, each thinking of the gift Oz had promised to bestow on him. Dorothy fell asleep only once, and then she dreamed she was in Kansas, where Aunt Em was telling her how glad she was to have her little girl at home again.

Promptly at nine o'clock the next morning the green-whiskered soldier came to them, and four minutes later they all went into the Throne Room of the Great Oz.

Of course each one of them expected to see the Wizard in the shape he had taken before, and all were greatly surprised when they looked about and saw no one at all in the room. They kept close to the door and closer to one another, for the stillness of the empty room was more dreadful than any of the forms they had seen Oz take.

Presently they heard a solemn Voice, that seemed to come from somewhere near the top of the great dome, and it said:

"I am Oz, the Great and Terrible. Why do you seek me?"

They looked again in every part of the room, and then, seeing no one,

Dorothy asked, "Where are you?"

"I am everywhere," answered the Voice, "but to the eyes of common mortals I am invisible. I will now seat myself upon my throne, that you may converse with me." Indeed, the Voice seemed just then to come straight from the throne itself; so they walked toward it and stood in a row while Dorothy said:

"We have come to claim our promise, O Oz."

"What promise?" asked Oz.

"You promised to send me back to Kansas when the Wicked Witch was destroyed," said the girl.

"And you promised to give me brains," said the Scarecrow.

"And you promised to give me a heart," said the Tin Woodman.

"And you promised to give me courage," said the Cowardly Lion.

"And you said you'd save the land from the horrible brain eaters," Dorothy concluded.

"Is the Wicked Witch really destroyed?" asked the Voice, and Dorothy thought it trembled a little.

"Yes," she answered, "I shot her and her dead slaves ate her."

"How did they eat her if they were dead?"

"Not really dead but the undead, as we've already discussed."

"Dear me," said the Voice, "how sudden! Well, come to me tomorrow, for I must have time to think it over."

"You've had plenty of time already," said the Tin Woodman angrily.

"We shan't wait a day longer," said the Scarecrow.

"You must keep your promises to us!" exclaimed Dorothy.

The Lion thought it might be as well to frighten the Wizard, so he gave a large, loud roar, which was so fierce and dreadful that Toto jumped away from him in alarm and tipped over the screen that stood in a corner. As it fell with a crash they looked that way, and the next moment all of them were filled with wonder. For they saw, standing in just the spot the screen had hidden, a little old man, with a bald head and a wrinkled face, who seemed to be as much surprised as they were. The Tin Woodman, raising his axe, rushed toward the little man and cried out, "Who are you?"

"I am Oz, the Great and Terrible," said the little man, in a trembling voice. "But don't strike me—please don't—and I'll do anything you want me to."

Our friends looked at him in surprise and dismay

"I thought Oz was a great Head," said Dorothy.

"And I thought Oz was a lovely Lady," said the Scarecrow.

"And I thought Oz was a terrible Beast," said the Tin Woodman.

"And I thought Oz was a Ball of Fire," exclaimed the Lion.

"No, you are all wrong," said the little man meekly. "I have been making believe."

"Making believe!" cried Dorothy. "Are you not a Great Wizard?"

"Hush, my dear," he said. "Don't speak so loud, or you will be overheard—and I should be ruined. I'm supposed to be a Great Wizard."

"And aren't you?" she asked.

"Not a bit of it, my dear; I'm just a common man."

"You're more than that," said the Scarecrow, in a grieved tone; "you're a humbug."

"Exactly so!" declared the little man, rubbing his hands together as if it pleased him. "I am a humbug."

"But this is terrible," said the Tin Woodman. "How shall I ever get my heart?"

"Or I my courage?" asked the Lion.

"Or I my brains?" wailed the Scarecrow, wiping the tears from his eyes with his coat sleeve.

"My dear friends," said Oz, "I pray you not to speak of these little things. Think of me, and the terrible trouble I'm in at being found out."

"Doesn't anyone else know you're a humbug?" asked Dorothy.

"No one knows it but you four—and myself," replied Oz. "I have fooled everyone so long that I thought I should never be found out. It was a great mistake my ever letting you into the Throne Room. Usually I will not see even my subjects, and so they believe I am something terrible."

"But, I don't understand," said Dorothy, in bewilderment. "How was it that you appeared to me as a great Head?"

"That was one of my tricks," answered Oz. "Step this way, please, and I will tell you all about it."

He led the way to a small chamber in the rear of the Throne Room, and they all followed him. He pointed to one corner, in which lay the great Head, made out of many thicknesses of paper, and with a carefully painted face.

"This I hung from the ceiling by a wire," said Oz. "I stood behind the screen and pulled a thread, to make the eyes move and the mouth open."

"But how about the voice?" she inquired.

"Oh, I am a ventriloquist," said the little man. "I can throw the sound of my voice wherever I wish, so that you thought it was coming out of the Head. Here are the other things I used to deceive you." He showed the Scarecrow the dress and the mask he had worn when he seemed to be the lovely Lady. And the Tin Woodman saw that his terrible Beast was nothing but a lot of skins, sewn together, with slats to keep their sides out. As for the Ball of Fire, the false Wizard had hung that also from the ceiling. It was really a ball of cotton, but when oil was poured upon it the ball burned fiercely.

"Really," said the Scarecrow, "you ought to be ashamed of yourself for being such a humbug."

"I am—I certainly am," answered the little man sorrowfully; "but it was the only thing I could do. Sit down, please, there are plenty of chairs; and I will tell you my story."

So they sat down and listened while he told the following tale.

"I was born in Omaha—"

"Why, that isn't very far from Kansas!" cried Dorothy.

"No, but it's farther from here," he said, shaking his head at her sadly. "When I grew up I became a ventriloquist, and at that I was very well trained by a great master. I can imitate any kind of a bird or beast." Here he mewed so like a kitten that Toto pricked up his ears and looked everywhere to see where she was. "After a time," continued Oz, "I tired of that, and became a balloonist."

"What is that?" asked Dorothy.

"A man who goes up in a balloon on circus day, so as to draw a crowd of people together and get them to pay to see the circus," he explained.

"Oh," she said, "I know."

"Well, one day I went up in a balloon and the ropes got twisted, so that I couldn't come down again. It went way up above the clouds, so far that a current of air struck it and carried it many, many miles away. For a day and a night I traveled through the air, and on the morning of the second day I awoke and found the balloon floating over a strange and beautiful country.

"It came down gradually, and I was not hurt a bit. But I found myself in the midst of a strange people, who, seeing me come from the clouds, thought I was a great Wizard. Of course I let them think so, because they were afraid of me, and promised to do anything I wished them to.

"Just to amuse myself, and keep the good people busy, I ordered them to build this City, and my Palace; and they did it all willingly and well. Then I thought, as the country was so green and beautiful, I would call it the Emerald City; and to make the name fit better I put green spectacles on all the people, so that everything they saw was green."

"But isn't everything here green?" asked Dorothy.

"No more than in any other city," replied Oz; "but when you wear green spectacles, why of course everything you see looks green to you. The Emerald City was built a great many years ago, for I was a young man when the balloon brought me here, and I am a very old man now. But my people have worn green glasses on their eyes so long that most of them think it really is an Emerald City, and it certainly is a beautiful place, abounding in jewels and precious metals, and every good thing that is needed to make one happy. I have been good to the people, and they like me; but ever since this Palace was built, I have shut myself up and would not see any of them.

"One of my greatest fears was the Witches, for while I had no magical powers at all I soon found out that the Witches were really able to do wonderful things. There were four of them in this country, and they ruled the people who live in the North and South and East and West. Fortunately, the Witches of the North and South were good, and I knew they would do me no harm; but the Witches of the East and West were terribly wicked, and had they not thought I was more powerful than they themselves, they would surely have destroyed me. As it was, I lived in deadly fear of them for many years; so you can imagine how pleased I was when I heard your house had fallen on the Wicked Witch of the East. When you came to me, I was willing to promise anything if you would only do away with the other Witch; but, now that you have killed her, I am ashamed to say that I cannot keep my promises."

"I think you are a very bad man," said Dorothy.

"Oh, no, my dear; I'm really a very good man, but I'm a very bad Wizard, I must admit."

"Can't you give me brains?" asked the Scarecrow.

"You don't need them. You are learning something every day. A baby has brains, but it doesn't know much. Experience is the only thing that brings knowledge, and the longer you are on earth the more experience you are sure to get."

"But no one wants to eat me, therefore I cannot really have brains."

"I understand, but knowledge comes in many forms, and with you it comes through the adventures you have survived."

"That may all be true," said the Scarecrow, "but I shall be very unhappy unless you give me brains."

The false Wizard looked at him carefully.

"Well," he said with a sigh, "I'm not much of a magician, as I said;

but if you will come to me tomorrow morning, I will stuff your head with brains. I cannot tell you how to use them, however; you must find that out for yourself."

"Oh, thank you—thank you!" cried the Scarecrow. "I'll find a way to use them, never fear!"

"But how about my courage?" asked the Lion anxiously.

"You have plenty of courage, I am sure," answered Oz. "All you need is confidence in yourself. There is no living thing that is not afraid when it faces danger. The true courage is in facing danger when you are afraid, and that kind of courage you have in plenty."

"Perhaps I have, but I'm scared just the same," said the Lion. "I shall really be very unhappy unless you give me the sort of courage that makes one forget he is afraid."

"Very well, I will give you that sort of courage tomorrow," replied Oz.

"How about my heart?" asked the Tin Woodman.

"Why, as for that," answered Oz, "I think you are wrong to want a heart. It makes most people unhappy. If you only knew it, you are in luck not to have a heart."

"That must be a matter of opinion," said the Tin Woodman. "For my part, I will bear all the unhappiness without a murmur, if you will give me the heart."

"Very well," answered Oz meekly. "Come to me tomorrow and you shall have a heart. I have played Wizard for so many years that I may as well continue the part a little longer."

"And how am I to get back to Kansas?" Dorothy asked.

"We shall have to think about that," replied the little man. "Give me two or three days to consider the matter and I'll try to find a way to carry you over the desert."

"And when I am gone, the ghastly dead Munchkins will go away?"

"Unfortunately no," said Oz. "But now that you have killed the Witch all we have to do is kill all the remaining creatures and in time this land will return to normal."

"That's not much of a solution," said Dorothy. "Their bite is infectious and they keep making new undead."

"I see your point. I never thought of that before. I shall have to think on all of these problems and get back to you. In the meantime you shall all be treated as my guests, and while you live in the Palace my people will wait upon you and obey your slightest wish. There is only one thing I ask in return for my help—such as it is. You must keep my secret and tell no one I am a humbug."

They agreed to say nothing of what they had learned, and went back to their rooms in high spirits. Even Dorothy had hope that "The Great and Terrible Humbug," as she called him, would find a way to solve their problems, and if he did she was willing to forgive him everything.

16
The Magic Art of
the Great Humbug

NEXT MORNING THE Scarecrow said to his friends:

"Congratulate me. I am going to Oz to get my brains at last. When I return I shall be as other men are."

"I have always liked you as you were," said Dorothy simply.

"It is kind of you to like a Scarecrow," he replied. "But surely you will think more of me when you hear the splendid thoughts my new brain is going to turn out." Then he said good-bye to them all in a cheerful voice and went to the Throne Room, where he rapped upon the door.

"Come in," said Oz.

The Scarecrow went in and found the little man sitting down by the window, engaged in deep thought.

"I have come for my brains," remarked the Scarecrow, a little uneasily.

"Oh, yes; sit down in that chair, please," replied Oz. "You must excuse me for taking your head off, but I shall have to do it in order to put your brains in their proper place."

"That's all right," said the Scarecrow. "You are quite welcome to take my head off, as long as it will be a better one when you put it on again."

So the Wizard unfastened his head and emptied out the straw. Then he entered the back room and took up a measure of bran, which he mixed with a great many pins and needles. Having shaken them together thoroughly, he filled the top of the Scarecrow's head with the mixture and stuffed the rest of the space with straw, to hold it in place.

When he had fastened the Scarecrow's head on his body again he said to him, "Hereafter you will be a great man, for I have given you a lot of bran-new brains."

The Scarecrow was both pleased and proud at the fulfillment of his greatest wish, and having thanked Oz warmly he went back to his friends.

Dorothy looked at him curiously. His head was quite bulged out at the top with brains.

"How do you feel?" she asked.

"I feel wise indeed," he answered earnestly. "When I get used to my brains I shall know everything."

"Why are those needles and pins sticking out of your head?" asked the Tin Woodman.

"That is proof that he is sharp," remarked the Lion.

"Well, I must go to Oz and get my heart," said the Woodman. So he walked to the Throne Room and knocked at the door.

"Come in," called Oz, and the Woodman entered and said, "I have come for my heart."

"Very well," answered the little man. "But I shall have to cut a hole in your breast, so I can put your heart in the right place. I hope it won't hurt you."

"Oh, no," answered the Woodman. "I shall not feel it at all."

So Oz brought a pair of tinsmith's shears and cut a small, square hole in the left side of the Tin Woodman's breast. Then, going to a chest of drawers, he took out a pretty heart, made entirely of silk and stuffed with sawdust.

"Isn't it a beauty?" he asked.

"It is, indeed!" replied the Woodman, who was greatly pleased. "But is it a kind heart?"

"Oh, very!" answered Oz. He put the heart in the Woodman's breast and then replaced the square of tin, soldering it neatly together where it had been cut.

"There," said he; "now you have a heart that any man might be proud of. I'm sorry I had to put a patch on your breast, but it really couldn't be helped."

"Never mind the patch," exclaimed the happy Woodman. "I am very grateful to you, and shall never forget your kindness."

"Don't speak of it," replied Oz.

Then the Tin Woodman went back to his friends, who wished him every joy on account of his good fortune.

The Lion now walked to the Throne Room and knocked at the door.

"Come in," said Oz.

"I have come for my courage," announced the Lion, entering the room.

"Very well," answered the little man; "I will get it for you."

He went to a cupboard and reaching up to a high shelf took own a square green bottle, the contents of which he poured into a green-gold dish, beautifully carved. Placing this before the Cowardly Lion, who sniffed at it as if he did not like it, the Wizard said:

"Drink."

"What is it?" asked the Lion.

"Well," answered Oz, "if it were inside of you, it would be courage. You know, of course, that courage is always inside one; so that this really cannot be called courage until you have swallowed it. Therefore I advise you to drink it as soon as possible."

The Lion hesitated no longer, but drank till the dish was empty.

"How do you feel now?" asked Oz.

"Full of courage," replied the Lion, who went joyfully back to his friends to tell them of his good fortune.

Oz, left to himself, smiled to think of his success in giving the Scarecrow and the Tin Woodman and the Lion exactly what they thought they wanted. "How can I help being a humbug," he said, "when all these people make me do things that everybody knows can't be done? It was easy to make the Scarecrow and the Lion and the Woodman happy, because they imagined I could do anything. But it will take more than imagination to carry Dorothy back to Kansas, and of these dreadful undead; I'm not sure there is anything more I can do."

17

How the Balloon Was Launched

For THREE DAYS Dorothy heard nothing from Oz. These were sad days for the little girl, although her friends were all quite happy and contented. The Scarecrow told them there were wonderful thoughts in his head; but he would not say what they were because he knew no one could understand them but himself. When the Tin Woodman walked about he felt his heart rattling around in his breast; and he told Dorothy he had discovered it to be a kinder and more tender heart than the one he had owned when he was made of flesh. The Lion declared he was afraid of nothing on earth, and would gladly face an army or a dozen of the fierce Kalidahs, Stappers, and even the undead.

Thus each of the little party was satisfied except Dorothy, who longed more than ever to get back to Kansas.

On the fourth day, to her great joy, Oz sent for her, and when she entered the Throne Room he greeted her pleasantly:

"Sit down, my dear; I think I have found the way to get you out of this country."

"And back to Kansas?" she asked eagerly.

"Well, I'm not sure about Kansas," said Oz, "for I haven't the faintest notion which way it lies. But the first thing to do is to cross the desert, and then it should be easy to find your way home."

"How can I cross the desert?" she inquired.

"Well, I'll tell you what I think," said the little man. "You see, when I came to this country it was in a balloon. You also came through the air, being carried by a cyclone. So I believe the best way to get across the desert will be through the air. Now, it is quite beyond my powers to make a cyclone; but I've been thinking the matter over, and I believe I can make a balloon."

"How?" asked Dorothy.

"A balloon," said Oz, "is made of silk, which is coated with glue to keep the gas in it. I have plenty of silk in the Palace, so it will be no trouble to make the balloon. But in all this country there is no gas to fill the balloon with, to make it float."

"If it won't float," remarked Dorothy, "it will be of no use to us."

"True," answered Oz. "But there is another way to make it float, which is to fill it with hot air. Hot air isn't as good as gas, for if the air should get cold the balloon would come down in the desert, and we should be lost."

"We!" exclaimed the girl. "Are you going with me?"

"Yes, of course," replied Oz. "I am tired of being such a humbug. If I should go out of this Palace my people would soon discover I am not a Wizard, and then they would be vexed with me for having deceived them. So I have to stay shut up in these rooms all day, and it gets tiresome. I'd much rather go back to Kansas with you and be in a circus again."

"I shall be glad to have your company," said Dorothy. But she could see something was not sincere with Oz, and while she had been taught not to question her elders, she feared that Oz was hiding something. "Is that why you really want to leave? Couldn't you just tell everyone that you were tricking them again with your real looks? They wouldn't be the wiser."

Oz hung his head, for he had been found out by this tiny girl. "My child, I must confess, there is more to my desire to leave. There have been reports of many undead marching toward the castle. I thought that if the Wicked Witch were killed these creatures would soon die off. But it seems you were right about their bites. There are more now than ever before, or so my reports tell me. I am sure they will soon take over the land and I don't want to be here anymore when that happens."

"So you are going to run away?"

"Well, aren't you as well? I do not see you offering to stay and help."

"But there is nothing I can do. I am just a little girl."

"A little girl who has now killed two witches, and from what I hear, many other dangerous creatures. You are quite gifted at killing that which threatens people harm."

"But I don't want to kill anymore. I am a nice person. I don't want to be covered in blood all the time."

"Then help me sew the silk together and we will begin to work on our balloon. Then we will both escape to freedom."

Dorothy felt ashamed to want to leave, but she could not deny her need to get back home. She was never meant for shooting guns and fighting witches. So she took a needle and thread, and as fast as Oz cut the strips of silk into proper shape the girl sewed them neatly together. First there was a strip of light green silk, then a strip of dark green and then a strip of emerald green; for Oz had a fancy to make the balloon in different shades of the color about them. It took three days to sew all the strips together, but when it was finished they had a big bag of green silk more than twenty feet long.

Then Oz painted it on the inside with a coat of thin glue, to make it airtight, after which he announced that the balloon was ready.

"But we must have a basket to ride in," he said. So he sent the soldier with the green whiskers for a big clothes basket, which he fastened with many ropes to the bottom of the balloon.

When it was all ready, Oz sent word to his people that he was going to make a visit to a great brother Wizard who lived in the clouds to help them fight the coming onslaught of dead Munchkins, Winkies, Monkeys, Stappers, Kalidahs and various other beasts. The news spread rapidly throughout the city and everyone came to see the wonderful sight.

Oz ordered the balloon carried out in front of the Palace, and the people gazed upon it with much curiosity. The Tin Woodman had chopped a big pile of wood, and now he made a fire of it, and Oz held the bottom of the balloon over the fire so that the hot air that arose from it would be caught in the silken bag. Gradually the balloon swelled out and rose into the air, until finally the basket just touched the ground.

Then Oz got into the basket and said to all the people in a loud voice:

"I am now going away to make a visit. While I am gone the Scarecrow will rule over you. I command you to obey him as you would me."

It was at this moment that a lone figure shambled out of a nearby alleyway and bit down hard on one of the castle guard's arms. The guard screamed and everyone turned to see one of the undead Munchkins tearing the guard's arm off.

"They've made it into the City," Oz said. "We are done for."

The Tin Woodman spun and fired a bullet between the eyes of the dead Munchkin, splitting its tiny head in two.

"And now that I have brains," said the Scarecrow, "I know that guard will soon die of infection and come back to eat us." So he fired a round from his own rifle into the guard's head. This angered the other guards, for they did not know of the infection, and were under the impression their new leader was a tyrant. Thus they began running away screaming that all was lost.

As they ran, more of the undead came out of the shadows and tackled them, gnawing their flesh off their bones. Screams of terror rose into the air, and Toto, sensing the excitement, raced out of Dorothy's arms to chase the undead.

The balloon was by this time tugging hard at the rope that held it to the ground, for the air within it was hot, and this made it so much lighter in weight than the air without that it pulled hard to rise into the sky.

"Come, Dorothy!" cried the Wizard. "Hurry up, or the balloon will fly away."

"I can't find Toto anywhere," replied Dorothy, who did not wish to leave her little dog behind. She saw him not far away, biting at the heels of a tiny Munchkin that was stuffing brains into its mouth. It was too occupied with its new kill, the body dead at its feet, to care about the dog.

"Quickly," shouted the Lion, who had joined in the fight and was swiping at one of the tiny blue decaying men trying to bite a lovely lady in a green dress. "Get in the basket and get out of here. You have helped us enough. It's time for you to leave."

Dorothy scooped up Toto and shot the dead Munchkin in the face. It fell down dead for real and the bullet continued out the back of its head, rose into the air, and opened a mouth that screamed such a loud wail that even the undead looked up to see what the commotion was. That was enough time for the Tin Woodman and Scarecrow to shoot them in the heads and kill them for good. Dorothy was within a few steps of the balloon now, and Oz was holding out his hands to help her into the basket, when, *crack!* went the ropes, and the balloon rose into the air without her.

"Come back!" she screamed. "I want to go, too!"

"I can't come back, my dear," called Oz from the basket. "Good-bye!"

All eyes were turned upward to where the Wizard was riding in the basket, rising every moment farther and farther into the sky. Hanging underneath it, their feet having gotten tangled in the ropes, were two undead Munchkins trying in vain to get up into the basket.

And that was the last any of them ever saw of Oz, the Wonderful Wizard, though he may have reached Omaha safely, and be there now, for all we know. But the people remembered him lovingly, and said to one another:

"Oz was always our friend. When he was here he built for us this beautiful Emerald City, and now he is gone he has left the Wise Scarecrow to rule over us."

Still, for many days they grieved over the loss of the Wonderful Wizard, and would not be comforted.

The Tin Woodman and Scarecrow were able to shoot the remaining undead, and as the sun fell, the Emerald City made sure to destroy the brains of all the creatures, and, sadly to destroy anyone who had been bitten.

18
Away to the South

DOROTHY WEPT BITTERLY at the passing of her hope to get home to Kansas again; but when she thought it all over she was glad she had not gone up in the balloon. And she also felt sorry at losing Oz, and so did her companions. But she wondered what would happen when he landed, and if the two Munchkins hanging under it would get him.

The Tin Woodman came to her and said:

"Truly I should be ungrateful if I failed to mourn for the man who gave me my lovely heart. I should like to cry a little because Oz is gone, if you will kindly wipe away my tears, so that I shall not rust."

"With pleasure," she answered, and brought a towel at once. Then the Tin Woodman wept for several minutes, and she watched the tears carefully and wiped them away with the towel. When he had finished, he thanked her kindly and oiled himself thoroughly with his jeweled oil-can, to guard against mishap.

The Scarecrow was now the ruler of the Emerald City, and although he was not a Wizard the people were proud of him, for they realized now he was trying to save them from the Wicked Witch's plague. "For," they said, "there is not another city in all the world that is ruled by a stuffed man who can wield a rifle with so much accuracy." And, so far as they knew, they were quite right.

The morning after the balloon had gone up with Oz, the four travelers met in the Throne Room and talked matters over. The Scarecrow sat in the big throne and the others stood respectfully before him.

"We are not so unlucky," said the new ruler, "for this Palace and the Emerald City belong to us, and we can do just as we please. When I remember that a short time ago I was up on a pole in a farmer's cornfield, and that now I am the ruler of this beautiful City, I am quite satisfied with my lot."

"I also," said the Tin Woodman, "am well-pleased with my new heart; and, really, that was the only thing I wished in all the world."

"For my part, I am content in knowing I am as brave as any beast that ever lived, if not braver," said the Lion modestly.

"But clearly there is a bigger problem, outside of the fact we still need to get Dorothy home, and that is the horrible dead men who want to eat us. As we have seen here, we will not be safe anywhere until they are destroyed."

"Well, then, what can be done?" inquired the Woodman.

The Scarecrow decided to think, and he thought so hard that the pins and needles began to stick out of his brains. Finally he said:

"Why not call the Winged Monkeys, and ask them to carry everyone to a new land, a land not cursed. And then they can carry you over the desert, Dorothy?"

"I never thought of that!" said Dorothy joyfully. "It's just the thing. I'll go at once for the Golden Cap."

When she brought it into the Throne Room she spoke the magic words, and soon the band of Winged Monkeys flew in through the open window and stood beside her.

"This is the second time you have called us," said the Monkey King, bowing before the little girl. He looked very tired and Dorothy could see that the battle with the Stappers had taken much out of him. "What do you wish?"

"I want you to fly everyone to safety, away from these dreadful creatures. Far away to another country. And you can take me over the desert and back to Kansas," said Dorothy.

But the Monkey King shook his head.

"That cannot be done," he said. "We belong to this country alone, and cannot leave it. There has never been a Winged Monkey outside of this land yet, and I suppose there never will be, for they don't belong anywhere else. We shall be glad to serve you in any way in our power, but we cannot take anywhere but within this land alone."

And with another bow, the Monkey King spread his wings and flew away through the window, followed by all his band.

Dorothy was ready to cry with disappointment. "I have wasted the charm of the Golden Cap to no purpose," she said, "for the Winged Monkeys cannot help me."

"It is certainly too bad!" said the tender-hearted Woodman.

The Scarecrow was thinking again, and his head bulged out so horribly that Dorothy feared it would burst.

"Let us call in the soldier with the green whiskers," he said, "and ask his advice."

So the soldier was summoned and entered the Throne Room timidly, for while Oz was alive he never was allowed to come farther than the door.

"We have a problem," said the Scarecrow to the soldier, "we must get Dorothy home and save this land from the curse of the dead. Who can help us with this?"

"I cannot tell," answered the soldier, "for nobody has ever left this land before, unless it is Oz himself. And no one has been able to put an end to the plague, only to re-kill a few here and there. I thought we were safe behind the walls of this City but that has been proven wrong. I wish I had a better answer."

"Is there no one who can help?" asked Dorothy earnestly.

"Glinda might," he suggested.

"Who is Glinda?" inquired the Scarecrow.

"The Witch of the South. She is the most powerful of all the Witches, and rules over the Quadlings. Besides, her castle stands on the edge of the desert, so she may know a way to cross it."

"Glinda is a Good Witch, isn't she?" asked the child.

"The Quadlings think she is good," said the soldier, "and she is kind to everyone. I have heard that Glinda is a beautiful woman, who knows how to keep young in spite of the many years she has lived."

"How can I get to her castle?" asked Dorothy.

"The road is straight to the South," he answered, "but, as you are now abundantly aware, it is full of dangers to travelers. There are more wild beasts in the woods, plenty of bloated and rotting little blue men, and to top it off, a race of queer men who do not like strangers to cross their country. For this reason none of the Quadlings ever come to the Emerald City."

The soldier then left them and the Scarecrow said:

"It seems, in spite of dangers, that the best thing Dorothy can do is to travel to the Land of the South and ask Glinda to help us. For, of course, if Dorothy stays here she will never get back to Kansas."

"You must have been thinking again," remarked the Tin Woodman.

"I have," said the Scarecrow.

"Well so have I," said Dorothy, "and it seems I am doomed to continually cross this land and face all of its dangers. I am quite annoyed with this."

"Yes, but you have a magic gun," said the Scarecrow, "and it has not failed you yet."

"I shall go with Dorothy," declared the Lion, "for I am tired of your city and long for the woods and the country again. I am really a wild beast, you know. I can handle myself if something bad comes along. Besides, Dorothy will need someone to protect her."

"That is true," agreed the Woodman. "My axe may be of service to her; so I also will go with you to the Land of the South."

"When shall we start?" asked the Scarecrow.

"Are you going?" they asked, in surprise.

"Certainly. If it wasn't for you all I should never have had brains. Dorothy lifted me from the pole in the cornfield and brought me to the Emerald City. So my good luck is all due to her, and I shall never leave her until she starts back to Kansas for good and all."

"Thank you," said Dorothy gratefully. "You are all very kind to me. But I should like to start as soon as possible."

"We shall go tomorrow morning," returned the Scarecrow. "So now let us all get ready, for it will be a long journey."

19
Attacked by the Fighting Trees

T HE NEXT MORNING Dorothy kissed the pretty green girl good-bye,
and they all shook hands with the soldier with the green whiskers, who
had walked with them as far as the gate. When the Guardian of the Gate
saw them again he wondered greatly that they could leave the relative
safety of the Emerald City to get into new trouble. But he at once
unlocked their spectacles, which he put back into the green box, and gave
them many good wishes to carry with them.

"You are now our ruler," he said to the Scarecrow; "so you must
come back to us as soon as possible."

"I certainly shall if I am able," the Scarecrow replied; "but there are
still problems to fix first."

As Dorothy bade the good-natured Guardian a last farewell she said:

"I have been very kindly treated in your lovely City, and everyone has
been good to me. I cannot tell you how grateful I am."

"Don't try, my dear," he answered. "We should like to keep you with
us, but if it is your wish to return to Kansas, I hope you will find a way."
He then opened the gate of the outer wall, and they walked forth and
started upon their journey.

The sun shone brightly as our friends turned their faces toward the
Land of the South. They were all in the best of spirits, and laughed and
chatted together. Dorothy was once more filled with the hope of getting
home, and the Scarecrow and the Tin Woodman were glad to be of use
to her. As for the Lion, he sniffed the fresh air with delight and whisked
his tail from side to side in pure joy at being in the country again, while
Toto ran around them and chased the moths and butterflies, barking
merrily all the time.

"City life does not agree with me at all," remarked the Lion, as they
walked along at a brisk pace. "I have lost much flesh since I lived there,
and now I am anxious for a chance to show the other beasts how
courageous I have grown."

They now turned and took a last look at the Emerald City. All they could see was a mass of towers and steeples behind the green walls, and high up above everything the spires and dome of the Palace of Oz.

"Oz was not such a bad Wizard, after all," said the Tin Woodman, as he felt his heart rattling around in his breast.

"He knew how to give me brains, and very good brains, too," said the Scarecrow.

"If Oz had taken a dose of the same courage he gave me," added the Lion, "he would have been a brave man."

Dorothy said nothing. Oz had not kept the promise he made her, but he had done his best, so she forgave him. As he said, he was a good man, even if he was a bad Wizard.

The first day's journey was through the green fields and bright flowers that stretched about the Emerald City on every side. They slept that night on the grass, with nothing but the stars over them; and they rested very well indeed.

In the morning they traveled on until they came to a thick wood. There was no way of going around it, for it seemed to extend to the right and left as far as they could see; and, besides, they did not dare change the direction of their journey for fear of getting lost. So they looked for the place where it would be easiest to get into the forest.

The Scarecrow, who was in the lead, finally discovered a big tree with such wide-spreading branches that there was room for the party to pass underneath. So he walked forward to the tree, but just as he came under the first branches they bent down and twined around him, and the next minute he was raised from the ground and flung headlong among his fellow travelers.

This did not hurt the Scarecrow, but it surprised him, and he looked rather dizzy when Dorothy picked him up.

"Here is another space between the trees," called the Lion.

"Let me try it first," said the Scarecrow, "for it doesn't hurt me to get thrown about." He walked up to another tree, as he spoke, but its branches immediately seized him and tossed him back again.

"This is strange," exclaimed Dorothy. "What shall we do?"

"The trees seem to have made up their minds to fight us, and stop our journey," remarked the Lion.

"I believe I will try it myself," said the Woodman, and shouldering his axe, he marched up to the first tree that had handled the Scarecrow so roughly. When a big branch bent down to seize him the Woodman chopped at it so fiercely that he cut it in two. From the severed limb thick black ooze shot out and pooled on the ground. At once the tree began shaking all its branches as if in pain, and the Tin Woodman passed safely under it.

"Come on!" he shouted to the others. "Be quick!" They all ran forward and passed under the tree without injury, except Toto, who was caught by a small branch and shaken until he howled. But the Woodman promptly chopped off the branch and set the little dog free.

They were halfway through the trees now when something large and purple hung down from the branches in front of them. It lifted an oblong head, opened bright red eyes, and stuck out a dark forked tongue.

"Snake," said the Lion.

But it was not just any Snake, Dorothy saw, but a Snake of immense size, large enough to swallow her whole. Its body was wrapped in a coil high up in the treetops, so large it practically blocked out the sun.

"How do we get by it?" Dorothy asked.

"You cannot get by me," the Snake replied. "No one ever gets by. If you come just one step closer I shall eat you alive."

Hearing this threat, the Tin Woodman raised his axe and took a step forward. "I will cut you in two if you try to harm us."

"I think not," said the Snake, and from the trees behind the travelers his long tail came down and scooped them all up. The four heroes, and even Toto, were wrapped so tightly they could not move let alone get to their weapons.

"Which one shall I eat first?" the Snake asked. "This Lion looks nice and meaty. I am sure he will fill my belly very nicely."

The Lion roared and said, "If you eat me I will claw my way to freedom from inside."

"You will be digested," replied the Snake. Its forked tongue darted out and licked the Lion's head. "Very tasty."

But just then the Lion bit the Snake's tongue and held it fast in his teeth. The Snake slithered wildly, howling in pain. "Let go of my tongue!"

"You let go of us first," cried Dorothy. "Hold it fast, Lion, until he drops us."

"Oh, I will drop you!"

At this point little Toto sank his tiny teeth into the Snake's skin and bit down hard. The Snake yelped again and withdrew into the treetops, taking the travelers up with him. When it was so very high up that Dorothy thought she could see over the whole Land of Oz, it dropped them onto the highest branch and backed away. The Lion let go, as did

Toto, and everyone sat on the branch wondering what to do.

"Now you are in my world," said the Snake, "and if you bite me again I will knock you all to the ground far below. Now I will slurp up your tender bodies."

The Snake slithered in close and looked right at Dorothy, but the Tin Woodman, being free from the Snake's tail, stepped in front of her. "Kiss my axe," he said, and swung it into the monster's head.

The Scarecrow aimed his rifle and joined in the fight as well. His bullet tore the Snake's tongue clean off, and if fell all the way down to the forest floor below. As the Tin Woodman hacked away, the Scarecrow shot more rounds into the scaly creature's head, eyes, mouth, and nose. What was once a magnificent reptilian visage was reduced to ground meat in seconds.

"Well, the Snake is dead," said Dorothy, "but how do we get down?"

"I have an idea," said the Scarecrow. "We can use the Snake like a giant rope and climb down him to the ground."

So that's exactly what they did. And when they go back to the ground, Dorothy kissed the Scarecrow for having such a wonderful idea.

Now, once again covered in a fresh collection of blood and dirt, they continued through the woods. The other trees of the forest did nothing to keep them back, so they made up their minds that only the first row of trees could bend down their branches, and that probably these were the policemen of the forest, and given this wonderful power in order to keep strangers out of it.

The four travelers walked with ease through the trees until they came to the farther edge of the wood. Then, to their surprise, they found before them a high wall which seemed to be made of white china. It was smooth, like the surface of a dish, and higher than their heads.

"What shall we do now?" asked Dorothy.

"I will make a ladder," said the Tin Woodman, "for we certainly must climb over the wall."

20

The Dainty China Country

WHILE THE WOODMAN was making a ladder from wood which he found in the forest Dorothy lay down and slept, for she was tired by the long walk. The Lion also curled himself up to sleep and Toto lay beside him.

The Scarecrow watched the Woodman while he worked, and said to him:

"I cannot think why this wall is here, nor what it is made of."

"Rest your brains and do not worry about the wall," replied the Woodman. "When we have climbed over it, we shall know what is on the other side."

After a time the ladder was finished. It looked clumsy, but the Tin Woodman was sure it was strong and would answer their purpose. The Scarecrow waked Dorothy and the Lion and Toto, and told them that the ladder was ready. The Scarecrow climbed up the ladder first, but he was so awkward that Dorothy had to follow close behind and keep him from falling off. When he got his head over the top of the wall the Scarecrow said, "Oh, my!"

"Go on," exclaimed Dorothy.

So the Scarecrow climbed farther up and sat down on the top of the wall, and Dorothy put her head over and cried, "Oh, my!" just as the Scarecrow had done.

Then Toto came up, and immediately began to bark, but Dorothy made him be still.

The Lion climbed the ladder next, and the Tin Woodman came last; but both of them cried, "Oh, my!" as soon as they looked over the wall. When they were all sitting in a row on the top of the wall, they looked down and saw a strange sight.

Before them was a great stretch of country having a floor as smooth and shining and white as the bottom of a big platter. Scattered around were many houses made entirely of china and painted in the brightest colors. These houses were quite small, the biggest of them reaching only as high as Dorothy's waist. There were also pretty little barns, with china fences around them; and many cows and sheep and horses and pigs and chickens, all made of china, were standing about in groups.

But the strangest of all were the people who lived in this queer country. There were milkmaids and shepherdesses, with brightly colored bodices and golden spots all over their gowns; and princesses with most gorgeous frocks of silver and gold and purple; and shepherds dressed in knee breeches with pink and yellow and blue stripes down them, and golden buckles on their shoes; and princes with jeweled crowns upon their heads, wearing ermine robes and satin doublets; and funny clowns in ruffled gowns, with round red spots upon their cheeks and tall, pointed caps. And, strangest of all, these people were all made of china, even to their clothes, and were so small that the tallest of them was no higher than Dorothy's knee.

No one did so much as look at the travelers at first, except one little purple china dog with an extra-large head, which came to the wall and barked at them in a tiny voice, afterwards running away again.

"How shall we get down?" asked Dorothy.

They found the ladder so heavy they could not pull it up, so the Scarecrow fell off the wall and the others jumped down upon him so that the hard floor would not hurt their feet. Of course they took pains not to light on his head and get the pins in their feet. When all were safely down they picked up the Scarecrow, whose body was quite flattened out, and patted his straw into shape again.

"We must cross this strange place in order to get to the other side," said Dorothy, "for it would be unwise for us to go any other way except due South."

They began walking through the country of the china people, and the first thing they came to was a china milkmaid milking a china cow. As they drew near, the cow suddenly gave a kick and kicked over the stool, the pail, and even the milkmaid herself, and all fell on the china ground with a great clatter.

Dorothy was shocked to see that the cow had broken her leg off, and that the pail was lying in several small pieces, while the poor milkmaid had a nick in her left elbow.

"There!" cried the milkmaid angrily. "See what you have done! My cow has broken her leg, and I must take her to the mender's shop and have it glued on again. What do you mean by coming here and frightening my cow?"

"I'm very sorry," returned Dorothy. "Please forgive us."

But the pretty milkmaid was much too vexed to make any answer. She picked up the leg sulkily and led her cow away, the poor animal limping on three legs. As she left them the milkmaid cast many reproachful glances over her shoulder at the clumsy strangers, holding her nicked elbow close to her side.

Dorothy was quite grieved at this mishap.

"We must be very careful here," said the kind-hearted Woodman, "or we may hurt these pretty little people so they will never get over it."

A little farther on Dorothy met a most beautifully dressed young Princess, who stopped short as she saw the strangers and started to run away.

Dorothy wanted to see more of the Princess, so she ran after her. But the china girl cried out:

"Don't chase me! Don't chase me!"

She had such a frightened little voice that Dorothy stopped and said, "Why not?"

"Because," answered the Princess, also stopping, a safe distance away, "if I run I may fall down and break myself."

"But could you not be mended?" asked the girl.

"Oh, yes; but one is never so pretty after being mended, you know," replied the Princess.

"I suppose not," said Dorothy.

"Now there is Mr. Joker, one of our clowns," continued the china lady, "who is always trying to stand upon his head. He has broken himself so often that he is mended in a hundred places, and doesn't look at all pretty. Here he comes now, so you can see for yourself."

Indeed, a jolly little clown came walking toward them, and Dorothy could see that in spite of his pretty clothes of red and yellow and green he was completely covered with cracks, running every which way and showing plainly that he had been mended in many places.

The Clown put his hands in his pockets, and after puffing out his cheeks and nodding his head at them saucily, he said:

"My lady fair,
Why do you stare
At poor old Mr. Joker?
You're quite as stiff
And prim as if
You'd eaten up a poker!"

"Be quiet, sir!" said the Princess. "Can't you see these are strangers, and should be treated with respect?"

"Well, that's respect, I expect," declared the Clown, and immediately stood upon his head.

"Don't mind Mr. Joker," said the Princess to Dorothy. "He is considerably cracked in his head, and that makes him foolish."

"Oh, I don't mind him a bit," said Dorothy. "But you are so beautiful," she continued, "that I am sure I could love you dearly. Won't you let me carry you back to Kansas, and stand you on Aunt Em's mantel? I could carry you in my basket."

"That would make me very unhappy," answered the china Princess. "You see, here in our country we live contentedly, and can talk and move around as we please. But whenever any of us are taken away our joints at once stiffen, and we can only stand straight and look pretty. Of course that is all that is expected of us when we are on mantels and cabinets and drawing-room tables, but our lives are much pleasanter here in our own country."

"I would not make you unhappy for all the world!" exclaimed Dorothy. "So I'll just say good-bye."

"Good-bye," replied the Princess.

They walked carefully through the china country. The little animals and all the people scampered out of their way, fearing the strangers would break them, and after an hour or so the travelers reached the other side of the country and came to another china wall.

It was not so high as the first, however, and by standing upon the Lion's back they all managed to scramble to the top. Then the Lion gathered his legs under him and jumped on the wall; but just as he jumped, he upset a china church with his tail and smashed it all to pieces.

All the tiny china people that were inside came stumbling out holding their broken limbs. There was even one little boy holding his own head in his hands. The head was crying quite mournfully. Others were trying to put their arms and legs back on but there was nothing to hold them in place. It was an awful sight to see.

"I am terribly sorry," said the Lion, jumping back down to see if he could help. But when he did, he landed on the town theater and shattered it to pieces. In the midst of this new destruction he saw even more little heads and limbs among the debris. Surely there would be no way to put some of these people back together.

Now the china people were getting quite upset indeed, and the china police showed up in a china carriage with a tiny china cannon on the end of it. "Death to the monsters," they cried, and fired china cannonballs at the Lion. But the cannon balls merely shattered upon impact and did not harm the Lion.

"I think you should leave now, Lion," said Dorothy. The Lion agreed and jumped back onto the wall, sad that he had destroyed so many people.

"That was too bad," said Dorothy, "but really I think we were lucky in not killing them all. They are all so brittle!"

"They are, indeed," said the Scarecrow, "and I am thankful I am made of straw and cannot be easily damaged. There are worse things in the world than being a Scarecrow."

21

The Lion Becomes the King of Beasts

AFTER CLIMBING DOWN from the china wall the travelers found themselves in a disagreeable country, full of bogs and marshes and covered with tall, rank grass. It was difficult to walk without falling into muddy holes, for the grass was so thick that it hid them from sight. However, by carefully picking their way, they got safely along until they reached solid ground. But here the country seemed wilder than ever, and after a long and tiresome walk through the underbrush they entered another forest, where the trees were bigger and older than any they had ever seen.

"This forest is perfectly delightful," declared the Lion, looking around him with joy. "Never have I seen a more beautiful place."

"It seems gloomy," said the Scarecrow.

"Not a bit of it," answered the Lion. "I should like to live here all my life. See how soft the dried leaves are under your feet and how rich and green the moss is that clings to these old trees. Surely no wild beast could wish a pleasanter home."

"Perhaps there are wild beasts in the forest now," said Dorothy.

"I suppose there are," returned the Lion, "but I do not see any of them about."

They walked through the forest until it became too dark to go any farther. Dorothy and Toto and the Lion lay down to sleep, while the Woodman and the Scarecrow kept watch over them as usual.

When morning came, they started again. Before they had gone far they heard a low rumble, as of the growling of many wild animals. Toto whimpered a little, but none of the others was frightened, and they kept along the well-trodden path until they came to an opening in the wood, in which were gathered hundreds of beasts of every variety. There were tigers and elephants and bears and wolves and foxes and all the others in the natural history, and for a moment Dorothy was afraid. But the Lion explained that the animals were holding a meeting, and he judged by their snarling and growling that they were in great trouble.

As he spoke several of the beasts caught sight of him, and at once the great assemblage hushed as if by magic. The biggest of the tigers came up to the Lion and bowed, saying:

"Welcome, O King of Beasts! You have come in good time to fight our enemy and bring peace to all the animals of the forest once more."

"What is your trouble?" asked the Lion quietly.

"We are all threatened," answered the tiger, "by a fierce enemy which has lately come into this forest. It is a most tremendous monster, like a great spider, with a body as big as an elephant and legs as long as a tree trunk. It has eight of these long legs, and as the monster crawls through the forest he seizes an animal with a leg and drags it to his mouth, where he eats it as a spider does a fly. Not one of us is safe while this fierce creature is alive, and we had called a meeting to decide how to take care of ourselves when you came among us."

The Lion thought for a moment.

"Are there any other lions in this forest?" he asked.

"No; there were some, but the monster has eaten them all. And, besides, they were none of them nearly so large and brave as you."

"If I put an end to your enemy, will you bow down to me and obey me as King of the Forest?" inquired the Lion.

"We will do that gladly," returned the tiger; and all the other beasts roared with a mighty roar: "We will!"

"Where is this great spider of yours now?" asked the Lion.

"Yonder, among the oak trees," said the tiger, pointing with his forefoot.

"Take good care of these friends of mine," said the Lion, "and I will go at once to fight the monster."

He bade his comrades good-bye and marched proudly away to do battle with the enemy.

The great spider was lying asleep when the Lion found him, and it looked so ugly that its foe turned up his nose in disgust. Its legs were quite as long as the tiger had said, and its body covered with coarse black hair. It had a great mouth, with a row of sharp teeth a foot long; but its head was joined to the pudgy body by a neck as slender as a wasp's waist. This gave the Lion a hint of the best way to attack the creature, and as he knew it was easier to fight it asleep than awake, he gave a great spring and landed directly upon the monster's back.

The Spider jerked awake at this and was very upset. "Who dares disturb my sleep?" it asked.

"It is I, Lion, King of Beasts."

"Ah, yes, I have heard of you. You are with the little girl that cut off my brother's legs."

The Lion remembered the story Dorothy had told him about the spider web she fell into and the big Spider that tried to eat her. "That was your brother? He tried to eat my friend. I am glad his legs are gone."

"And I am glad you have come to wake me, for I was very hungry."

"I must warn you I have faced bigger dangers than you and am well prepared to fight you and free this forest from your rule."

"So be it," said the Spider, and charged at the Lion. But you will remember that the Lion was full of courage now, and he charged at the Spider in return. They met in a roaring crash and rolled over one another on the forest floor. The Spider drove its fangs into the Lion's sides but the Lion was quick and jumped away before the Spider's poison could be injected. The Lion then hit the Spider in its many eyes with a mighty blow from his paw. Several of the Spider's eyes exploded in a syrup of dark blood while others merely dangled by veins. "I cannot see!" the Spider screamed.

This was good news for the Lion, whose sides stung from the puncture wounds inflicted by the monster's fangs. He climbed up onto the Spider's back and bit down hard, opening up a deep wound from which flowed even more blood. This did not deter the Spider, who began shooting strands of silk everywhere in the hopes of harnessing the Lion.

"You will not stop me," roared the Lion, and bit down again, using his vicious teeth to tear open a wide hole in the Spider's head. For the Lion knew that if he was going to truly kill this creature he had to kill the brain, otherwise it would come back from the dead. He drove his massive claws into the Spider's skull and found the creature's brain. With a mighty roar he yanked it out and threw it against a tree, where it splattered and slid down the bark to the ground. The Spider fell in a heap and the Lion jumped off just as its legs curled in, almost trapping him.

He watched it for a few minutes, just to make sure it was truly dead. When he knew it wasn't going to come back to life, the Lion went back to the opening where the beasts of the forest were waiting for him and said proudly:

"You need fear your enemy no longer."

The Tiger helped Dorothy and her friends clean the Lion's wounds, and after he was rested they began on their journey again. Before they left, the beasts bowed down to the Lion as their King, and he promised to come back and rule over them as soon as Dorothy was safely on her way to Kansas.

22

The Country of the Quadlings

THE FOUR TRAVELERS passed through the rest of the forest in safety, and when they came out from its gloom saw before them a steep hill, covered from top to bottom with great pieces of rock.

"That will be a hard climb," said the Scarecrow, "but we must get over the hill, nevertheless."

So he led the way and the others followed. They had nearly reached the first rock when they heard a rough voice cry out, "Keep back!"

"Who are you?" asked the Scarecrow.

Then a head showed itself over the rock and the same voice said, "This hill belongs to us, and we don't allow anyone to cross it."

"But we must cross it," said the Scarecrow. "We're going to the country of the Quadlings."

"But you shall not!" replied the voice, and there stepped from behind the rock the strangest man the travelers had ever seen.

He was quite short and stout and had a big head, which was flat at the top and supported by a thick neck full of wrinkles. But he had no arms at all, and, seeing this, the Scarecrow did not fear that so helpless a creature could prevent them from climbing the hill. So he said, "I'm sorry not to do as you wish, but we must pass over your hill whether you like it or not," and he walked boldly forward.

As quick as lightning the man's head shot forward and his neck stretched out until the top of the head, where it was flat, struck the Scarecrow in the middle and sent him tumbling, over and over, down the hill. Almost as quickly as it came the head went back to the body, and the man laughed harshly as he said, "It isn't as easy as you think!"

A chorus of boisterous laughter came from the other rocks, and Dorothy saw hundreds of the armless Hammer-Heads upon the hillside, one behind every rock.

The Lion became quite angry at the laughter caused by the Scarecrow's mishap, and giving a loud roar that echoed like thunder, he dashed up the hill.

Again a head shot swiftly out, and the great Lion went rolling down the hill as if he had been struck by a cannon ball.

Dorothy ran down and helped the Scarecrow to his feet, and the Lion came up to her, feeling rather bruised and sore, and said, "It is useless to fight people with shooting heads; no one can withstand them."

"Oh, I have had it," said Dorothy, and unslung her magic rifle. "No more Mrs. Nice Girl." She fired at each of the Hammer-Heads and blew their skulls high up into the air. The Scarecrow and Tin Woodman followed suit and shot them as well. All of the strangers' heads were blown clean into the sky and their bodies fell down in bloody heaps.

Awash in Hammer-Head blood, Dorothy shouldered her weapon and proudly crossed the hill. She kicked one of the bodies as she went, just to make a point. "Hit me with your head now, jerk. If you can find it."

The country of the Quadlings seemed rich and happy. There was field upon field of ripening grain, with well-paved roads running between, and pretty rippling brooks with strong bridges across them. The fences and houses and bridges were all painted bright red, just as they had been painted yellow in the country of the Winkies and blue in the country of the Munchkins. The Quadlings themselves, who were short and fat and looked chubby and good-natured, were dressed all in red, which showed bright against the green grass and the yellowing grain.

The travelers came to a farmhouse, and the four travelers walked up to it and knocked at the door. It was opened by the farmer's wife, and when Dorothy asked for something to eat the woman gave them all a good dinner, with three kinds of cake and four kinds of cookies, and a bowl of milk for Toto.

"How far is it to the Castle of Glinda?" asked the child.

"It is not a great way," answered the farmer's wife. "Take the road to the South and you will soon reach it.

Thanking the good woman, they started afresh and walked by the fields and across the pretty bridges until they saw before them a very beautiful Castle. Before the gates were three young girls, dressed in handsome red uniforms trimmed with gold braid; and as Dorothy approached, one of them said to her:

"Why have you come to the South Country?"

"To see the Good Witch who rules here," she answered. "Will you take me to her?"

"Let me have your name, and I will ask Glinda if she will receive you." They told who they were, and the girl soldier went into the Castle. After a few moments she came back to say that Dorothy and the others were to be admitted at once.

23

Glinda the Good Witch Grants Dorothy's Wish

BEFORE THEY WENT to see Glinda, however, they were taken to a room of the Castle, where Dorothy washed her face and combed her hair, and the Lion shook the dust out of his mane and changed the bandages on his wounds, and the Scarecrow patted himself into his best shape, and the Woodman polished his tin and oiled his joints.

When they were all quite presentable they followed the soldier girl into a big room where the Witch Glinda sat upon a throne of rubies.

She was both beautiful and young to their eyes. Her hair was a rich red in color and fell in flowing ringlets over her shoulders. Her dress was pure white but her eyes were blue, and they looked kindly upon the little girl.

"What can I do for you, my child?" she asked.

Dorothy told the Witch all her story: how the cyclone had brought her to the Land of Oz, how she had found her companions, and of the wonderful adventures they had met with.

"My greatest wish now," she added, "is to get back to Kansas, for Aunt Em will surely think something dreadful has happened to me, and that will make her put on mourning; and unless the crops are better this year than they were last, I am sure Uncle Henry cannot afford it. But I am afraid I made a promise to the Good Witch of the North that I must still fulfill, for if were to leave now I would leave my friends here with a terrible curse to continue dealing with."

"And what is that promise, my dear?"

"To put an end to the Wicked Witch of the West's spell that raises the dead."

"Yes, I know well of that curse," said Glinda. "It has plagued us as horribly. Unfortunately I cannot break another witch's spell."

"I know this," said Dorothy, "but now that the Wicked Witch

is dead—"

"Dead? How did she die?"

"I shot her and her slaves ate her," Dorothy replied.

"Well, that is a different story," said Glinda. "If she is dead then all we have to do is kill every last undead beast and all will return to normal."

"But that's impossible, there are too many of them. They keep biting people and making more. Even Oz couldn't solve that problem."

"Then we will need plenty of weapons. Come with me." Glinda led the travelers to a big room in her Castle where there were more weapons than anyone could count. There were rifles and pistols and canons and swords and axes and shields and shotguns and strange guns Dorothy could not even place.

"We will make a stand," said Glinda. "With everyone working together we can rid the land of every last undead being. We will gather all of our friends and fight together."

"But the creatures are all over the place," said the Scarecrow. "It will take forever to find them all."

"Not with magic," said Glinda. "I will make the biggest brain you have ever seen and fly it high over Munchkin Land. It will smell like brain and look like brain and be a beacon to every abomination in the land. When they come to eat it, we will kill them. Will you fight?"

Everyone said they would, and they each grabbed a handful of guns and swords to take back to Munchkin Land. When they had stocked up and put on suits of armor, Glinda waved her wand over everyone and they suddenly found themselves standing back where Dorothy had first arrived in this strange country. Her house was still where it had landed, and the roads were still bloodstained from the first battle she witnessed. The Good Witch of the North was there and was happy to hear that everyone had come to wage war.

For the next several days Dorothy, the Scarecrow, the Tin Woodman, the Lion and Glinda coached everyone on how to fight. Dorothy used the Golden Cap to call the Flying Monkeys, and having one last command for them, asked them to help fight as well. The King pledged his allegiance to the battle, saying he was tired of the dangers that roamed the country. Glinda visited all of the nearby lands and told them of the battle they were preparing for. Soon the Guardian of the Gate arrived, as did the Winkies, the Tiger from the forest, and even the Queen of the Field Mice, who came with hundreds of her family. Many farmers arrived with their own weapons such as scythes and rakes and hoes and helped build blockades. Together, everyone worked to stronghold the houses. The Munchkins were so happy to have friends willing to help put an end to the curse that had been plaguing them that they threw a party for Dorothy and called her their hero.

24

The Battle for Oz

DAYS LATER, AFTER the Munchkin Land was fortified and booby trapped, Glinda created a giant brain out of thin air and let it rise many hundreds of feet into the air for all the land to see. The smell of the meat was strong, and even the Lion said it made him hungry.

The first undead appeared over the hills a few hours later. This group of undead Munchkins stared up at the brain in the sky and came forward with loud moans. "Braiiins."

When they got close, Dorothy, who was positioned on top of a tiny Munchkin house, shot her magic gun at them. The bullet formed a net that lifted the undead high into the air and dropped them down onto jagged rocks, shattering their skulls and exploding their brains out of their heads.

"Here comes another wave," the Tin Woodman yelled. Indeed more undead Munchkins had arrived from the woods. He fired with startling precision and shot them in the head.

"More over there," said the Lion, referring to the undead Munchkins coming out of the cornfields. He stood proudly in front of a group of farmers, each with a gun from Glinda's armory. "Remember to aim for the head."

Guns began to fire everywhere, and the smell of gunpowder grew very thick. Tiny undead Munchkin heads blossomed into clouds of red mist. The Tin Woodman and the Scarecrow were the best shots, hitting the undead between the eyes most of the time. Little Toto, who was wearing a small suit of doggy armor they'd found in Glinda's armory, ran out into the streets and started tripping the undead. When they fell Dorothy would shoot them. Glinda and the Witch of the North shot bolts of fire at the undead, burning them alive.

"More coming," shouted the King of the Monkeys. He and his fellow Monkeys flew up into the air to meet the flying undead Monkeys that had been turned during their fight with the Stappers. They divebombed each other, throwing punches and biting at each other's heads and bodies. Dorothy had given the King and his band guns to use, and as they swooped and barrel-rolled they fired at the heads of their former mates. Monkey brains rained down on the houses below, splattering loudly in wet piles of mush.

Meanwhile, the undead mice began to scurry out of the grasses and make their way inside the houses, looking for a way up to the giant brain. Often they would settle on trying to bite a Munchkin or farmer, but the Queen of the Field Mice was prepared for them and had her best warriors lying in wait for them. Each tiny mouse had a small cannon fitted to its back which it could fire by pulling the tiny string that hung down from it. Thus, inside the houses the sounds of tiny pops and snaps echoed off the walls as undead mice met their fate.

The Lion and Tiger raced down the middle of the street, biting off the legs of the undead so that the others could take the creatures' heads off with gunfire. Dorothy managed to kill twenty with one super magical bullet that blew ice onto them all, freezing them solid before it came back again to shatter them into shards that melted into water.

But two of the rotted blue creatures had somehow gotten onto the roof with her and knocked her down. She felt tiny Munchkin teeth scraping against the armor she wore. "Help!" she cried. "Help!"

And suddenly Boq was there was the scythe he used to tend his wheat, and he hacked off the creatures' heads and kicked them off the roof. He handed Dorothy back her gun and said, "I will watch your back from now on, little child. Just keep shooting."

Dorothy thanked him and trained her gun on the mob of undead in the street below. Everywhere blue men and yellow men and red men clashed, spilling blood in magnificent amounts. Tiny severed arms and legs and heads grew into large mounds as the inhabitants of this magical land took it back from the walking dead.

In the air the monkeys had beaten off all of their undead kin, and now the dead Monkeys lay broken on the ground with bullet holes in their Monkey brains. The King and his followers flew back down to the surrounding trees and sniped at the shambling Munchkins and Winkies moaning in the fields.

Over the course of the next many hours more undead creatures arrived, including crows and rabbits and even Stappers, which the Good Witches of the North and South took care of by magically removing their wings so that they fell out of the sky and got smashed to pulp on the ground.

The Scarecrow and Tin Woodman stood back to back in the middle of the Yellow Brick Road and fired with expert marksmanship at anything that got close.

"Good shot, Scarecrow," the Tin Woodman said.

"Excellent shot, yourself," replied the Scarecrow. Soon they were nearly surrounded by a circular wall of dead creatures. The Tin Woodman had to use his axe to hack a path through the pile of bodies.

"They really want to eat me this time," the Scarecrow said. "My new brains really are magnificent."

The Guardian of the Gate had been put in charge of demolitions, and was busy igniting bombs in places where they had corralled the undead. Little blue, rotting men went flying through the air to land in thick puddles of goo. He kept his Emerald glasses on and remarked at the amount of green blood everywhere.

The battle lasted for many days, and the Munchkins took turns sleeping while others fought. Dorothy took a nap on the roof, holding Toto in her arms, who had been brought back to her by the King of the Monkeys. The little doggie was tired from biting all of the undeads' feet and tripping them over.

At one point Dorothy awoke at night to watch the Witches shooting fire and light at the massive waves of undead that streamed out of the woods. For as far as Dorothy's eyes could see, the brain-eaters stretched on forever, up over hills and into the trees and out past the cornfields, which were steadily burning.

She could see the Yellow Brick Road from up here, and felt bad that it was nothing but a pile of rubble now, covered with limbs.

Dorothy awoke several more times and joined back in the battle, always amazed at how her gun never ran out of ammunition. The bullets did such magical things before killing the walking corpses. One bullet turned into a raven that pecked its beak into the heads of the undead, ripping out their brains. Another bullet turned to rope and tied up the creatures so others could shoot them. One even shrank the creatures to such a small size that the Queen of the Field Mice and her followers were able to tear their heads off.

Through day and night everyone battled. Occasionally a Winkie or Munchkin would get bit, but the warriors had all formed a pact before the battle began that anyone who got bitten must be shot. And so it was sad to hear of the few brave soldiers that had to be put down, but Dorothy knew it was better than if they came back to eat brains.

On the morning the battle ended, Dorothy awoke to the sounds of laughter and singing birds. She peered over the edge of the roof and found herself staring into the glazed eyes of a Munchkin head. But it was just a head without a body. It was sitting atop of pile of limbs that had grown so high it was almost taller than the house. Dorothy scooped up Toto and walked down the pile of limbs as if they were stairs. She gasped at the sight around her.

Smoke from dying fires rose gently into the air. The trees had been felled and lay atop many dead bodies. The Monkey King was helping to bandage up his fellow Monkeys, many of whom had broken limbs. The Queen of the Field Mice was resting in between the Lion's paws, who was himself snoring soundly. The Tin Woodman and Scarecrow were still wide awake, for they did not need to sleep, and both were busy helping the Witches pile up the dead bodies. Many houses had been destroyed, and just about everything was awash in blood. In fact, the Scarecrow was so bloody he had asked the Tin Woodman to wipe off his eyes so he could see. Now his entire face was just a red stain with two eyes.

Dorothy stepped over many limbs and severed heads and found herself climbing up another mound of bodies. When she reached the top she held her gun up high and waved to the Witches.

"Did we do it?" she asked.

Everyone in the streets stopped to look at her, for the little girl was so beautiful in her bloodstained armor, holding her little dog in one arm and her gun in the other, standing on top of a plague they had now defeated. Her silver shoes were now completely ruby colored, stained with the blood of the fallen.

With a resounding cry the entire town threw their hands up and cheered for Dorothy, for it was she who had united the land against the Wicked Witch of the West's curse. If she had not arrived, they would still be battling for their lives.

"Long live Dorothy!" they shouted. "Queen of Oz!"

Now the Lion awoke, and he and the Scarecrow and the Tin Woodman rushed up to hug her. They hugged her for so very long and Dorothy felt tears of joy running down her face.

"You did it, Dorothy," said the Lion.

"No, you did it, Lion, with your courage. And you, Scarecrow, with your brains. And you, Tinman, with your heart."

"You all did it," said Glinda, who floated up to the top of the pile of bodies. The Good Witch of the North joined them as well. "We all did it," she added.

Glinda leaned forward and kissed the sweet, upturned face of the loving little girl. "Bless your dear heart," she said. "I shall be sad to see you go."

Dorothy felt herself stop breathing for a moment. "Do you mean you will tell me how I can get back to Kansas?"

"I am sure I can tell you of a way to get back to Kansas." Then she added, "But, if I do, you must give me the Golden Cap."

"Willingly!" exclaimed Dorothy; "indeed, it is of no use to me now, and when you have it you can command the Winged Monkeys three times."

"And I think I shall need their service just those three times," answered Glinda, smiling.

Dorothy then gave her the Golden Cap, and the Witch said to the Scarecrow, "What will you do when Dorothy has left us?"

"I will return to the Emerald City," he replied, "for Oz has made me its ruler and the people like me. The only thing that worries me is how to cross the hill of the Hammer-Heads, for I think it is time for me to stop killing."

"By means of the Golden Cap I shall command the Winged Monkeys to carry you to the gates of the Emerald City," said Glinda, "for it would be a shame to deprive the people of so wonderful a ruler."

"Am I really wonderful?" asked the Scarecrow.

"You are unusual," replied Glinda.

Turning to the Tin Woodman, she asked, "What will become of you when Dorothy leaves this country?"

He leaned on his bloodstained axe and thought a moment. Then he said, "The Winkies were very kind to me, and wanted me to rule over them after the Wicked Witch died. I am fond of the Winkies, and if I could get back again to the Country of the West, I should like nothing better than to rule over them forever."

"My second command to the Winged Monkeys," said Glinda "will be that they carry you safely to the land of the Winkies. Your brain may not be so large to look at as those of the Scarecrow, but you are really brighter than he is—when you are well polished—and I am sure you will rule the Winkies wisely and well."

Then the Witch looked at the big, shaggy Lion and asked, "When Dorothy has returned to her own home, what will become of you?"

"Over the hill of the Hammer-Heads," he answered, "lies a grand old forest, and all the beasts that live there have made me their King. If I could only get back to this forest, I would pass my life very happily there."

"My third command to the Winged Monkeys," said Glinda, "shall be to carry you to your forest. Then, having used up the powers of the Golden Cap, I shall give it to the King of the Monkeys, that he and his band may thereafter be free for evermore."

The Scarecrow and the Tin Woodman and the Lion now thanked the Good Witch earnestly for her kindness; and Dorothy exclaimed:

"You are certainly as good as you are beautiful! But you have not yet told me how to get back to Kansas."

"Your Silver . . . er . . . Ruby Shoes will carry you over the desert," replied Glinda. "If you had known their power you could have gone back to your Aunt Em the very first day you came to this country."

"But then I should not have had my wonderful brains!" cried the Scarecrow. "I might have passed my whole life in the farmer's cornfield."

"And I should not have had my lovely heart," said the Tin Woodman. "I might have stood and rusted in the forest till the end of the world."

"And I should have lived a coward forever," declared the Lion, "and no beast in all the forest would have had a good word to say to me."

"And we would all be slaves to the undead curse," exclaimed the Witch of the North.

"This is all true," said Dorothy, "and I am glad I was of use to everyone. But now that each of you has had what you most desired, and each is happy in having a kingdom to rule besides, I think I should like to go back to Kansas."

"The Shoes," said the Good Witch, "have wonderful powers. And one of the most curious things about them is that they can carry you to any place in the world in three steps, and each step will be made in the wink of an eye. All you have to do is to knock the heels together three times and command the shoes to carry you wherever you wish to go."

"If that is so," said the child joyfully, "I will ask them to carry me back to Kansas at once."

She threw her arms around the Lion's neck and kissed him, patting his big head tenderly. Then she kissed the Tin Woodman, who was weeping in a way most dangerous to his joints. But she hugged the soft, stuffed body of the Scarecrow in her arms instead of kissing his painted face, and found she was crying herself at this sorrowful parting from her loving comrades.

Glinda the Good stepped down from her ruby throne to give the little girl a good-bye kiss, and Dorothy thanked her for all the kindness she had shown to her friends and herself.

Dorothy now took Toto up solemnly in her arms, and having said one last good-bye she clapped the heels of her shoes together three times, saying:

"Take me home to Aunt Em!"

Instantly she was whirling through the air, so swiftly that all she could see or feel was the wind whistling past her ears.

The Silver and Red Shoes took but three steps, and then she stopped so suddenly that she rolled over upon the grass several times before she knew where she was.

At length, however, she sat up and looked about her.

"Good gracious!" she cried.

For she was sitting on the broad Kansas prairie, and just before her was the new farmhouse Uncle Henry built after the cyclone had carried away the old one. Uncle Henry was milking the cows in the barnyard, and Toto had jumped out of her arms and was running toward the barn, barking furiously.

Dorothy stood up and found she was in her stocking-feet. For the Magical Shoes had fallen off in her flight through the air, and were lost forever in the desert.

25

Home Again

AUNT EM HAD just come out of the house to water the cabbages when she looked up and saw Dorothy running toward her.

"My darling child!" she cried, folding the little girl in her arms and covering her face with kisses. "Where in the world did you come from?"

"From the Land of Oz," said Dorothy gravely. "And here is Toto, too. And oh, Aunt Em! I'm so glad to be at home again!"

That night Dorothy slept soundly in her room with Toto curled up beside her. She thought of her friends in Oz and how wonderful they had all been to her. She would like to see that wonderful land again someday. Somehow, she knew she would. She fell asleep and had such lovely dreams.

Meanwhile, out by the barn, a small mouse with glazed eyes squeaked out of the bloodstained dress Aunt Em had taken from Dorothy to be thrown out. The mouse had such a hungry belly and thirst for brains that it bit each horse and pig it could find before scampering off across the gray prairie to the next town, where it finally found itself a tasty meal in the form of a sleeping hobo.

About the Authors

Ryan C. Thomas is an award-winning journalist and editor living in San Diego, California. You can usually find him in the bars on the weekends playing with his band, The Buzzbombs. When he is not writing or rocking out, he is at home with his cat, Elvis, watching really bad B-movies. Visit him online at **www.ryancthomas.com**

L. Frank Baum was born in 1856 and died in 1919. He was a prolific author, using both his name and several pen names. He is best known, however, for the numerous books all taking place in the Land of Oz, *The Wonderful Wizard of Oz* being his most famous.

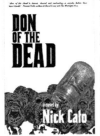
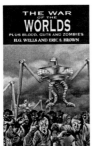

THE PLACE TO GO FOR ZOMBIE AND APOCALYPTIC FICTION

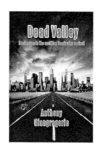

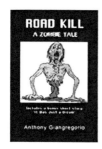

LIVING DEAD PRESS
WHERE THE DEAD WALK
www.livingdeadpress.com

CPSIA information can be obtained at www.ICGtesting.com
Printed in the USA
LVOW080516050612

284674LV00001B/116/P

9 781926 712178